D1020121

THE GREAT CAT CONSPIRACY

Katie Davies

Illustrated by Hannah Shaw

Beach Lane Books
New York London Toronto Sydney New Delhi

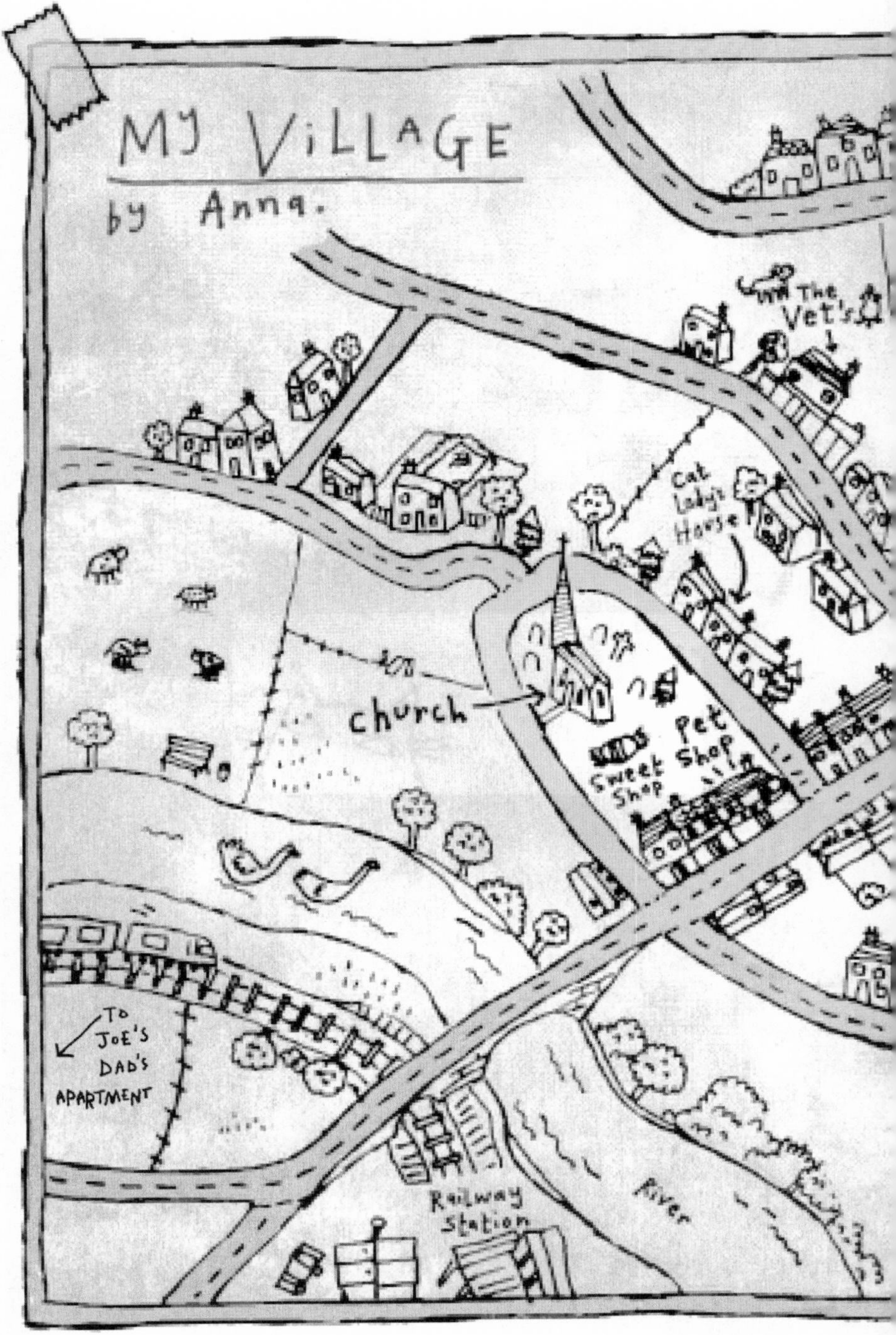

MY VILLAGE

by Anna.

The Vet's

Cat Lady's House

church

Pet Shop

Sweet Shop

TO JOE'S DAD'S APARTMENT

Railway Station

River

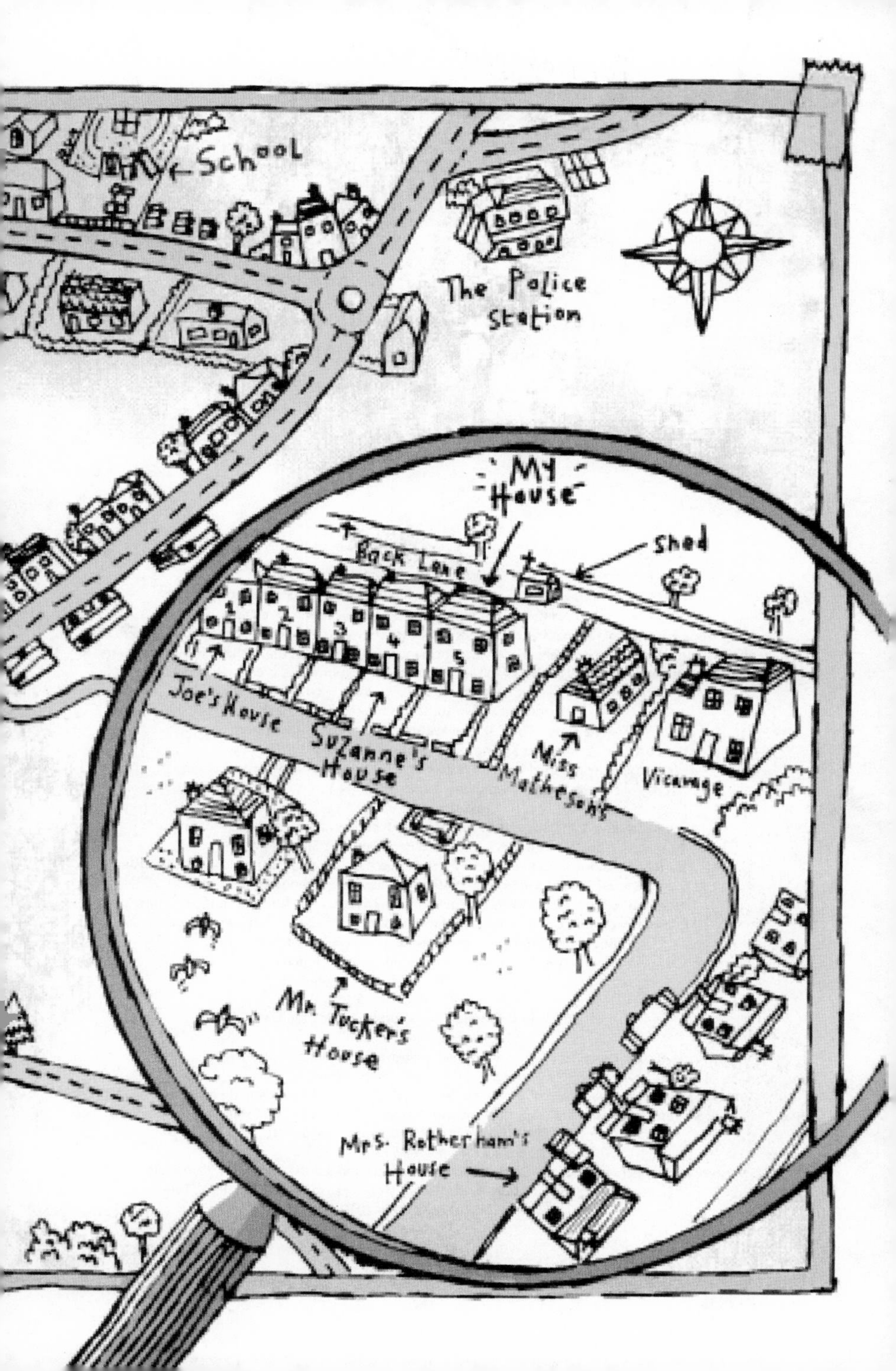
School
The Police Station
My House
Back Lane
Shed
1
2
3
4
5
Joe's House
Suzanne's House
Miss Matheson's
Vicarage
Mr. Tucker's House
Mrs. Rotherham's House

Thanks to Alan, and Mum and Dad,
and Venetia at Simon and Schuster.

BEACH LANE BOOKS
An imprint of Simon & Schuster Children's Publishing Division
1230 Avenue of the Americas, New York, New York 10020

The story "The Cat That Walked by Himself" is taken from
Rudyard Kipling's *Just So Stories*, published 1902.
Originally published in Great Britain in 2011 by Simon & Schuster UK Ltd.
Published by arrangement with Simon & Schuster UK Ltd
First U.S. edition 2012

Manufactured in the United States of America
0312 FFG
2 4 6 8 10 9 7 5 3 1
Library of Congress Cataloging-in-Publication Data
Davies, Katie, 1978–
The great cat conspiracy / Katie Davies ; illustrated by Hannah Shaw.—1st U.S. ed.
p. cm.—(The great critter capers)
Summary: When their naughty cat disappears while being disciplined for bringing home the head of the vicar's most expensive koi carp, three siblings suspect a kidnapping and start an investigation.
ISBN 978-1-4424-4513-0 (paper over board)
ISBN 978-1-4424-4515-4 (eBook)
[1. Mystery and detective stories. 2. Cats—Fiction. 3. Brothers and sisters—Fiction. 4. Family life—England—Fiction. 5. England—Fiction. 6. Humorous stories.] I. Shaw, Hannah, ill. II. Title.
PZ7.D283818Gp 2012
[Fic]—dc23
2011045508

CHAPTER 1

Cat Conspiracy

This is a story about Tom, and the Cat Lady, and everything that happened when the New Cat vanished. After it went missing, Mom said that me and Tom had to stop talking about the New Cat, and telling everyone how it had been kidnapped by the Cat Lady, and all that. She said, "*Anna*," (that's my name) "you can't go around accusing old ladies, and bandying words like 'conspiracy' about, which you don't even understand." But, like I told Tom, I *did* understand what a conspiracy was. Because me and my friend Suzanne looked it up in my dictionary, when we first heard there was one from Graham Roberts at Sunday School. This is what it said:

conspiracy [kun-spir-uh-see] ✦ *noun*
an evil, unlawful, treacherous, or surreptitious plan formulated in secret; plot

And what the dictionary said was probably right. Because ours wasn't the only cat that had vanished. Emma Hendry, in Mrs. Peters's class, couldn't find her cat either. And nor could Joe-down-the-street's babysitter, Brian. And Graham Roberts said he had *seen* the Cat Lady kidnapping cats, and taking them into her house, himself.

And he said, "With my *very own eyes,*" and swore it was true on Mrs. Constantine's *life*. Mrs. Constantine is in charge at Sunday School. She is the Vicar's wife.

Suzanne said that Graham swearing on Mrs. Constantine might not count, because Graham sometimes lies. And you're only supposed to swear on the life of someone you *like*. And Graham didn't even have Mrs. Constantine going to heaven when he did his big collage called "IT'S *JUDGEMENT* DAY!" Because he made her out of an egg carton and she was too big to fit on it.

Anyway, like I told Mom, me and Tom did know *some* things about the Cat Lady, and where the New Cat was, and what had happened to it, and so did Suzanne. Because we were the ones who had sent out the Search Party. *And* we were the ones who were actually *in* it. And the whole *point* of a Search Party is to find things out.

It was Tom who first noticed that the New Cat had vanished. Tom is my brother. He's five. He's four years younger than I am. I'm nine. I've got another brother and a sister too, called Andy and Joanne, but they're not in this story because they're older than me and Tom and they don't really care about cats or conspiracies or anything like that.

If it wasn't for Tom, no one might even have minded that the New Cat had gone anywhere. Because, before we couldn't find it, Tom was the only one in our house who cared about the New Cat, and what it got up to.

Mom said that *she* cared about what the New Cat got up to as well because, she said, "*I'm* the one who has to clean up after it all the time."

But that isn't really the same kind of caring.

Most cats don't need to be cleaned up after. That's why Mom said we could get a new one, after our *Old* Cat died, and why we weren't allowed a dog, like me and Tom wanted. The New Cat isn't like most cats, though. The New Cat makes more mess than anyone's dog does. It makes more mess even than Tom. And it's not easy-to-clean-up mess, either. Not like jigsaws, and sticklebricks, and Spider-Man pants, and all that. The mess that the New Cat makes is normally *dead*. Because, whenever it leaves the house, the New Cat *hunts.* And, after it's been hunting, it brings the things it has hunted inside, and puts them in places for people to find. Sometimes the things it brings in are still a bit alive.

Like the hedgehog curled up in a ball, which it rolled in through the front door. And the greenfinch with one wing, which was flapping behind the fridge. And the frog in the log basket, which me and Suzanne were going to bury, until we got it in the garden and it hopped out of its box.

Most of the time, though, the things that the New Cat

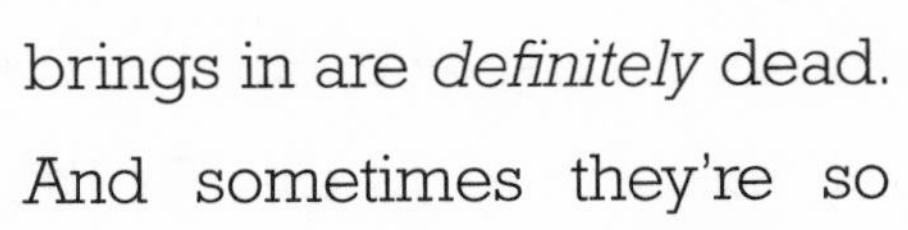

brings in are *definitely* dead. And sometimes they're so

dead it's hard to tell what they *would* have been when they were *alive*. And that's when you only find a few feathers, or a bunch of bones, or a pile of slimy insides.

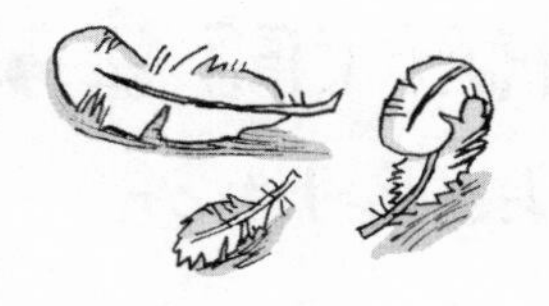

CHAPTER 2

The Petition

Suzanne lives next door. Her bedroom is right next to mine. If there wasn't a wall between our houses, our family and Suzanne's would live in one big house together, instead of two small houses apart, which would be a lot better. Because then me and Suzanne wouldn't have to ring on each other's doorbells, or bang on the wall, or shout through the letter box every time we needed to talk. We could talk all the time, whenever we wanted, while we're supposed to be doing other things, like brushing our teeth, or remembering our spelling, or staying in our rooms until we've thought about what we've done.

I asked Mom if we could knock down the wall between our house and Suzanne's house.

Mom laughed, even though it wasn't funny, and said, "You and Suzanne practically live together already." Which isn't true because we only have our dinner together on Tuesdays and Thursdays. And we aren't allowed to stay round each other's houses on school nights. And we don't go swimming together because Suzanne's got grommets.

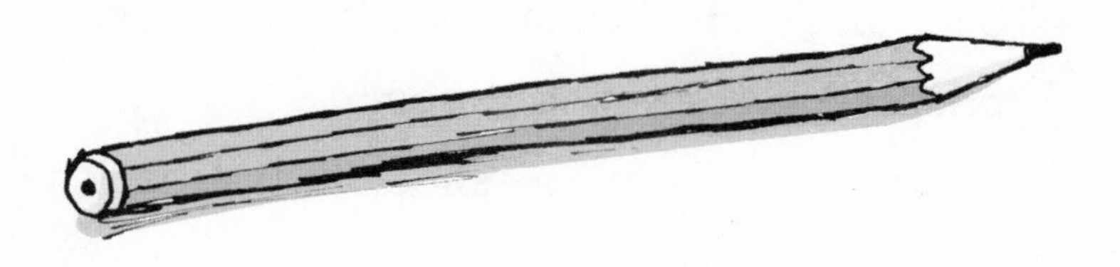

This is what it says about "grommets" in my dictionary:

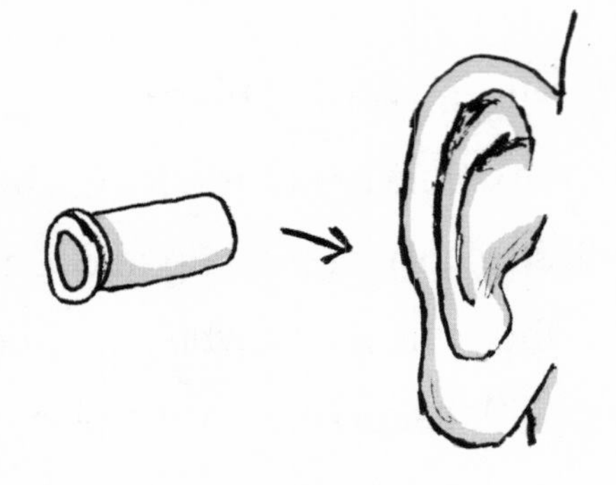

grommet [grom-it] ✦ *noun*
a tube-shaped device used for the treatment of persistent middle-ear infections where thick gluelike fluid builds up behind the eardrum

So me and Suzanne decided to do a Petition to see if we could get the wall knocked down that way, because, like Suzanne said, "When you do a Petition, people can see you're serious."

So we went in the shed, in the back

lane, which only me and Suzanne are allowed into (except for Tom if he wants, when he remembers the password), and Suzanne wrote "Purtishun" at the top of a piece of paper. And then she stopped because she said before she *wrote* the Purtishun, she just wanted to check exactly what one *was*. So we looked it up in the dictionary (which took a long time because Suzanne wasn't exactly sure how to spell it, either). This is what it said in my dictionary:

petition [puh-tish-un] ✦ *noun*
a formal request addressed to a person or persons in power, soliciting some favor, right, mercy, or other benefit

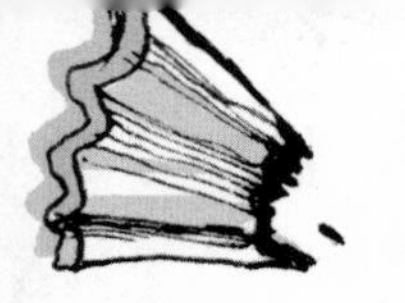

And this is what it said in Suzanne's:

petition [puh-tish-un] ✦ *noun*
a document signed by a large number of people demanding some action from the authorities

And, after that, we knew *exactly* what a petition was. And Suzanne said we could probably write one by ourselves, but just in case we might miss something out, we should go and see Mrs. Rotherham up the road. Mrs. Rotherham is really old. Her house smells a bit strange, of old things and mothballs, like Nana's house used to. But she's good at playing cards, and getting everyone ice cream, and showing you how to do things when you aren't exactly sure.

Mrs. Rotherham said, "A Petition? Sounds

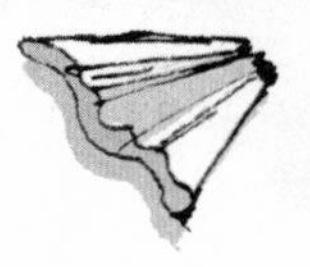

serious. You'd better come in."

So we did. And we told her all about the wall, and how we thought it would be better if it wasn't there, because we couldn't talk to each other through it anymore, not since Suzanne's Dad took Suzanne's walkie-talkie off her, in the middle of the night, and rang on our doorbell in his dressing gown, and made Mom get me out of bed, and said, **"*HAND* THE DAMN THING *OVER!* IF I HEAR, *'ANNA TO SUZANNE . . . ANNA TO SUZANNE,'* ONE MORE TIME, I'LL GO OUT OF MY *MIND!*"**

Mrs. Rotherham listened and said, *"Well,"* and, "I *see*," and, "Oh *dear*, oh dear, oh dear." And she said she thought a Petition was *just* what was called for. And that she would start us off, and me and Suzanne could finish.

This is what our Petition said:

We the undersigned (which Mrs. Rotherham said means "we the people who have signed this underneath") *are in agreement that the wall between the Morris house* (which is mine) *and the Barry house* (which is Suzanne's) *should be torn down in the name of peace and unity* and because it gets in the way and stops you being able to talk when you really need to, like in the middle of the night, when you aren't allowed out, and you haven't got walkie-talkies anymore, and you've thought of something important, which can't wait until the morning in case you forget it.

The people we got to sign it were . . .

A Morris (me)
S Barry (Suzanne)
K Rotherham (Mrs. Rotherham)
CB (Carl Barry, Suzanne's brother)

Suzanne's Mom said Carl's signature didn't count because he's only a baby, and he can't write, and Suzanne must have held his hand. Which Suzanne admitted afterward that she did, but only a bit.

We didn't exactly get a *large* number of people to sign the Petition, like Suzanne's dictionary said we should. Because getting people to put their names on was harder than we thought. Dad wouldn't sign it, and nor would Andy, or Joanne.

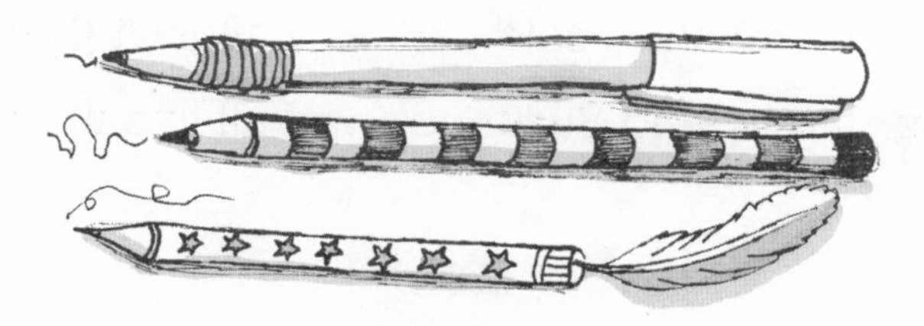

Even Tom wouldn't put his name on. And you can normally get Tom to do anything, as long as you give him a cookie.

I showed Tom the Petition, and the cookie, and he looked at it for ages. And then he said, "What does it say?" Because he's only five and he can't really read yet, except for "the," and "cat," and his name. So I read the Petition out loud, and Tom asked, "What does it mean?" So I told him how it was a serious thing, which people were putting their names on, to say they wanted the wall knocked down.

"What wall?"

"*This* one."

"Why?"

"Because," I said, "if the wall isn't there, our family and Suzanne's will all live in one *big* house, which would be a lot better."

Tom said, "Where will Suzanne's Dad live?"

Suzanne told Tom her Dad would live in the house as well.

But Tom said he didn't want to live with Suzanne's Dad because "he shouts too much." Which is true. We hear him all the time through the wall, when he's **"COUNTING TO *THREE*"** and when he's **"NOT GOING TO SAY IT *AGAIN*"** and when he's **"LOSING THE WILL TO *LIVE*!"**

Suzanne said she didn't think her Dad would shout at anyone on *our* side of the house, because he will only be in charge of the people on *her* side.

But Tom wasn't sure. And he said he would rather keep the wall where it was. Because some of it was in his bedroom, and it had his bookshelf on it, and his Batman stickers, and the bit he had colored in black with a crayon. And he went and asked Dad for a cookie instead.

I didn't say anything to Suzanne, but Tom was probably right about living with her Dad. And how he would be in charge.

Like he was the time our family and Suzanne's family went on a walk, which no one wanted to go on. He was definitely in charge of everyone then. Because he had a map, and a compass, and a stick that turned into a seat, which we weren't allowed to touch. And he told us what everything was, and how long it had been there. Like the bridge, and the battlements, and the boulders.

And there wasn't enough time to stop and play Pooh Sticks. And he walked in front and said, **"ONLY NINE MORE MILES,"** and **"WE WON'T BE BEATEN BY A BIT OF RAIN,"** and **"RUN FOR COVER, FOR CRYING OUT LOUD!"**

And he made Tom leave all his best things behind, which he had been collecting on the way, like a brick, and a sheet of blue plastic, and a bag of gravel. Because he said Tom was slowing us down.

And after that Tom refused to walk at all, and he lay facedown on the wet ground, and had what Nana used to call the Screaming Habdabs. And Dad had to carry him the whole way home.

Anyway, it probably wouldn't have made any difference *how* many people me and Suzanne had got to sign the Petition. Because when I showed it to Mom, she said,

"Don't be ridiculous, Anna. The wall is not coming down. This is a dictatorship, not a democracy. Get that eggplant eaten."

This is what it says a dictatorship is in my dictionary:

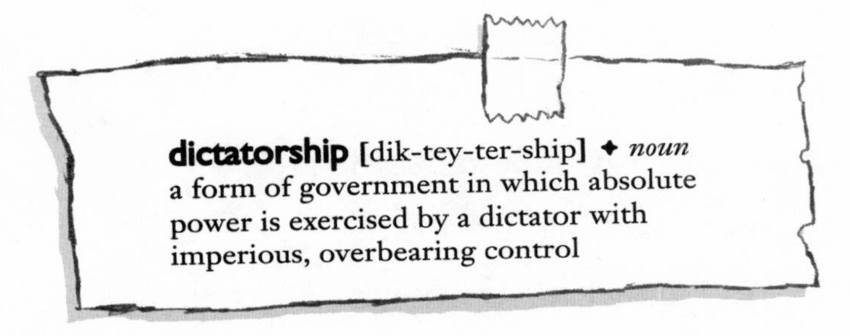

dictatorship [dik-tey-ter-ship] ✦ *noun*
a form of government in which absolute power is exercised by a dictator with imperious, overbearing control

And this is what it says a "democracy" is:

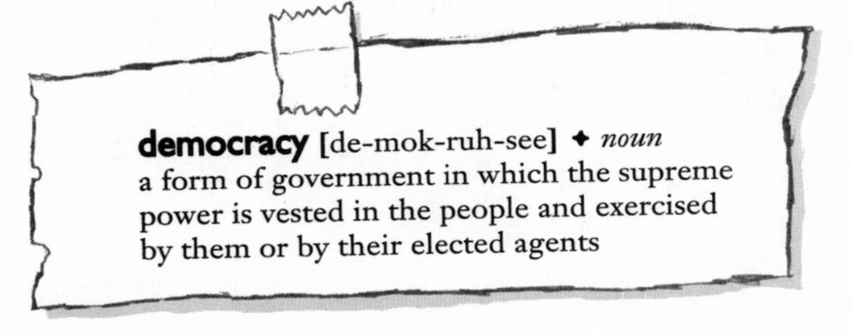

democracy [de-mok-ruh-see] ✦ *noun*
a form of government in which the supreme power is vested in the people and exercised by them or by their elected agents

I hate eggplant. Especially the ones from Suzanne's Dad's garden. Anyway, I stopped

wanting to get the wall down so much after that because for one thing, I thought Tom might be right about living with Suzanne's Dad, and for another thing, I found out that the wall had a *hole* in it.

CHAPTER 3
Three Blind Mice

The day I found out about the hole in the wall there was a strange smell in the house, like there is sometimes, when Mom stops what she's doing, and sniffs, and says, "*Ooh,* what on *earth* is *that*?"

And Dad says, "What?"

And Mom says, "I can *smell* something. Can't you?"

And Dad says, "Nope." And stares at the TV and tries not to talk about it.

And Mom goes sniffing round the house, on her hands and knees, until she finds out what it is. Sometimes it might be a moldy potato in the bottom of the vegetable rack. Or dog poo that came in on someone's shoe, and got trod into the carpet. But most of the time it's something that's dead somewhere, which the New Cat has dragged in from outside.

Mom followed the smell into the hall, until she came to the closet under the stairs, where the laundry basket is, and the ironing pile, and all Dad's things, at the back, that aren't really allowed to be there, like the bag of worn-out footballs, and the broken tennis rackets, and the pile of newspapers he hasn't got round to reading yet. The closet under the stairs has got so much

stuff in it that when you open the door, all the ironing falls out. And then you have to pick it all up, and shove it back in, and close the door quick, and put the catch down to keep it in. The closet under the stairs didn't *used* to have as much ironing in it as it does now. Because, before Nana died, whenever she came round, she always said, "My program's on in a bit. Get me set up, Duck, and I'll attack your ironing pile."

And then Mom got the ironing board out. And put it up in front of the TV. And Nana ironed everything, even things that Mom said were daft, like dishcloths, and hankies, and Tom's underwear. Because no one can iron as fast as Nana could, or as neatly. And at the end of *Coronation Street*, Nana stopped ironing and sat down. And Mom brought her half a cup of tea, in a china cup (because Nana didn't like mugs and she said if she had more than half a cup, she would be up and down to the toilet all night).

Anyway, this time, Mom was sniffing around. And when she came to the closet under the stairs, she stopped. And she opened the door. And all the ironing fell out. And she sniffed again, and said, "Oh no, it's coming from in *here*."

She sniffed through the ironing. And then she got the dirty laundry basket out, and sniffed through that. (I wouldn't sniff the things in the laundry basket because it's full of old football socks, and gymnastics leotards, and Dad's dirty pants, but Mom doesn't mind because she's a mom and that's what they do.)

And, after that, Mom started pulling Dad's things out of the closet as well, so she could get right inside. And she piled them all up in the hall. There was the alarm clock that doesn't go off, and the toaster that doesn't pop, and the kettle that me and Tom blew up by mistake.

Mom said, "No wonder there's not enough room for the ironing. It's like the electrical afterlife in here." And she pulled out some more stuff. A stool with one leg, and a bucket with a hole in the bottom, and half a broom handle without a head.

Me and Tom sat on the stairs and watched. And Mom said, "I thought I threw those out *years* ago." And, "Why on *earth* are we keeping *these*?" And, "*That's* as much use as a chocolate teapot."

After a while, there was so much stuff in the hall that you could hardly see the carpet. When Mom got to the very bottom of the closet, she found a black trash bag. And she sniffed inside. And then she put her

hand over her mouth, and made a sound like she was about to be sick, which went, "Eur-*ugh*-eka!"

And she put a pair of rubber gloves on, and laid some newspaper on the floor. And she reached inside the trash bag, and started pulling things out, one at a time.

The bag was full of Dad's clothes from the olden days, like we've seen in photos, from before he was even bald. There was a flowery shirt with a flappy collar, and some purple velvet flares, like Willy Wonka wears, and some massive underpants, with brown-and-orange stripes and a flap at the front, called Y-fronts.

Tom wanted to pull something out of the bag himself, because, he said, "It's a *lucky dip*."

But Mom said, "No! There's nothing

lucky about it. Stand *back*, Tom. It stinks!"

And she reached in again, and felt around, and she pulled something out, and held it up in the air, by its tail, and she said, *"Aha,* a *mouse*!" And she laid it on the newspaper. And then she tipped the trash bag upside down. And two more things fell out. And they were mice as well. Mom laid them on the newspaper, next to the first one.

Tom asked, "Are they dead?"

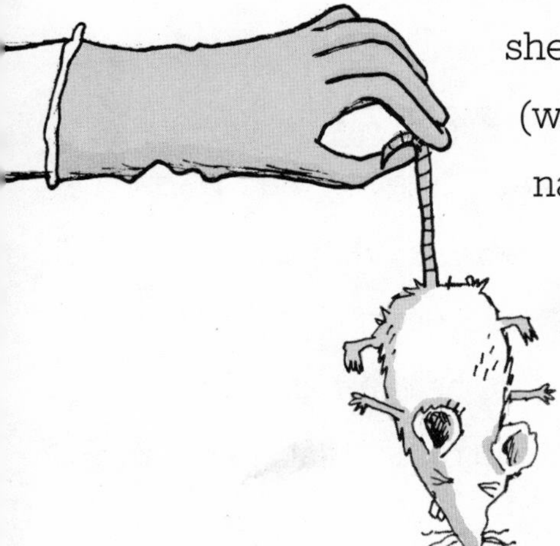

"*Dead?*" Mom said. "They're practically decomposed!" And then she shouted, *"PETE!"* (which is our Dad's name). Dad put the TV on pause and came into the hall. Mom pointed to the newspaper with the mice on it, in a line. And she said, "*What* do you call *this*?"

Dad said, "Urm . . . Three Blind Mice?" And he got The Hysterics (which is what you get when you start laughing and then you can't stop). And I got The Hysterics a bit as well. But Tom didn't, because he said he didn't think three blind mice were very funny, especially not when they were dead as well.

And neither did Mom, because she said, "It's a mass grave, Pete, for goodness' sake! The New Cat is disposing of its bodies in your trash bag."

And she told Dad to start sorting all his stuff out, under the stairs, like she had been asking him to "for *ten years*!" Because, she said, it was a breeding ground for bacteria, and a serious health hazard, and she had seen something on TV that said you shouldn't have anything in your house that isn't beautiful or useful.

And Dad said, "Well, we'd better get rid of Anna in that case." And he got The Hysterics again. But only a bit. Because nobody else did.

Mom said, "I mean it. Two piles: one for the dump and the other for the charity shop. I'm going to see Pam. I want it gone when I get back."

Pam is Joe-down-the-street's Mom. She lives with Joe and Joe's New Rabbit at number 1.

And Tom went as well. Tom loves it at Pam's house, even on the weekends when Joe's at his Dad's and it's just Mom and Pam, drinking tea and talking about boring things. Like work, and laundry, and Joe's Mom's New Boyfriend. Tom sits on Pam's knee and stays quiet, and eats all the cookies.

I didn't want to go to Pam's. And sorting things into piles and throwing them out isn't the kind of thing Dad is very good at, so I said I would stay and help. Because putting things in the trash is one of Dad's worst things. That's why he eats all the leftovers off my and Tom's plates, which is good when it's eggplant, and Mom hasn't noticed, or the black bit in our bananas, or the skin off our fish. Dad eats the bits that no one wants, even when he's already full up himself. And then he says, "Ugh, I've *eaten* too much," and has to go and lie down, in the dark, on the sofa, because he's too sick to help with the dishes.

CHAPTER 4
The Hole in the Wall

Dad looked at all the things in the hall. And he started putting them into two piles. And, after a while, he said that instead of *two* piles, he would do *three*: one for the charity shop, one for the dump, and one for things that might come in useful. And he said we wouldn't need to tell Mom about the *third* pile because we could put it all up in the loft. In secret.

So I held each thing up, and said what it was. Like, "a clock with no hands," and "an umbrella with a hole in it," and "a shoe with no sole." And Dad said which pile it should go in.

"Dump. No, charity shop. No, keep. Just *in case*."

When we had finished, there was a small pile for the charity shop. And a small pile for the dump. And a BIG pile of "useful" things to keep. And Dad said we had to hurry up and get the "useful" pile up into the loft before Mom came back.

So he got the stepladder from the shed, and took it up to my room, where the hatch for the loft is. And he climbed up and opened it. And some dust, and dirt, and dead flies fell out on his head.

And I went downstairs and got as many things as I could carry from the "useful" pile in the hall, and brought them back up, and passed them to Dad on the ladder. And I ran up and down doing that, as fast as I could. Because Dad said if we got it all done before Mom came back, he would let me go up the ladder, into the loft, myself.

Without getting off the ladder, Dad balanced all the things on top of one another, close to the loft hatch. And when he was finished, he let me go up.

Dad handed me his flashlight. I had never been in the loft before. It was dark, and dusty, and Dad said there were bats. And he said you have to be careful to walk on the beams. Otherwise you can come straight through the ceiling.

"Quick, Anna, before Mom comes. And don't knock anything. If that stuff falls through, my life won't be worth living."

Careful not to knock Dad's pile of things, and holding on to the beams above me, I stepped from beam to beam toward a wall I could see across the other side. On my left the roof got lower and lower, and on my right higher and higher. I reached the far wall, and ran my hand along. My hand went through a hole where some bricks were missing, and I grazed my arm.

"Hurry up!" Dad called out. "Don't go too far back."

I shone my flashlight through the hole. I could see beams and boxes, just like in our loft. Only these boxes were all in rows, and they were on top of boards that had been put down.

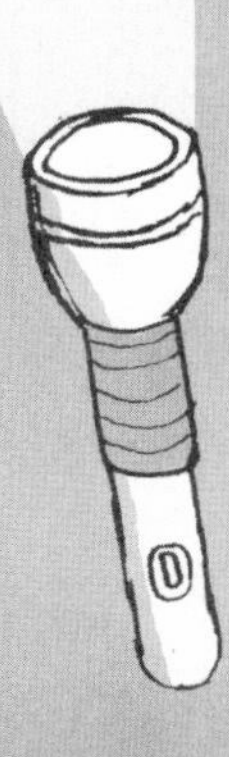

"All right, come back now, Anna."

I stuck my head right through

the hole, and squinted to see. Some of the boxes had writing on them. There were "Christmas Decorations," and "Camping Equipment," and one of the boxes said "Suzanne's old toys," in Suzanne's handwriting. The hole went straight into *Suzanne's* loft.

"Anna!" said Dad. "If you don't come back now, I'm closing the hatch."

I went back the way I had come, and careful not to touch Dad's pile of useful things, I followed him back down the ladder.

"What were you doing?" Dad said.

"Urm, I saw a bat," I said. And I slid down the ladder, and ran downstairs.

"Oi, I thought we were going to the dump? Wash your hands before Mom gets back. *Anna?*"

But I didn't answer. And I didn't have time to wash my hands. And I hadn't seen a bat. I needed to see Suzanne to tell her about the hatch, and the loft, and the wall, and the hole.

I ran round to her house. And I rang on the Barrys' doorbell three times. Me and Suzanne always do three rings if it's something important.

And then I ran away again because it was a Saturday, which meant Suzanne's Dad would be home, and he doesn't like people ringing the doorbell more than once. He sticks his head out the window and says, **"YES? IS THERE A FIRE? I HEARD IT THE *FIRST TIME*, FOR *CRYING OUT LOUD*!"**

I waited in the shed until Suzanne came round. And I told her all about the hatch, and the loft, and the wall, and the hole.

"We need to do a plan," Suzanne said. So we did. This is what the plan looked like when it was finished:

Since then, whenever me and Suzanne really need to talk, like in the middle of the night, when we aren't allowed out, and we've thought of something important, which can't wait until the morning, in case we forget it, I knock on Suzanne's wall three times, and if the coast is clear, Suzanne knocks back three times on mine. And then I climb up on my chest of drawers, and Suzanne climbs up on her wardrobe, and we reach up to the ceiling, and push the hatches back. And pull ourselves up on our arms, and scramble up inside. And we turn on our flashlights, and hold them between our teeth, because we need both hands to hold on to the roof, to balance from beam to beam, so we don't fall through the ceiling. And then we feel along the wall, and we meet at the hole. And we stay up there and talk about things, like the beams, and the bats, and whether there are holes in all the walls, in all the lofts, the whole way down the road. And how, if there are, you could climb through each one, and come out at the house at the bottom, which is Joe-down-the-street's.

CHAPTER 5

Miss Matheson's Dog

Before the New Cat vanished, when it wasn't busy hunting, and killing things, and hiding their bodies round the house, it used to follow Tom around and watch what he was doing. Most of the things Tom does aren't that good for watching, like walking in a straight line with his eyes closed, or collecting gravel, or helping Mr. Tucker pick up litter. But the New Cat didn't mind. It just waited nearby, with one eye open, watching Tom, and washing its whiskers.

Mr. Tucker lives on the other side of the road, in the house opposite. When he was young, Mr. Tucker was important in the Second World War, flying planes, and fighting enemies, and getting shot at, and all that. He's got lots of medals, and a pair of flying goggles with the glass smashed, and an old parachute to prove it. Mr. Tucker doesn't fight enemies anymore. He's too old. (Unless they've been throwing their beer cans into Mrs. Tucker's chrysanthemums.)

Mr. Tucker was there when the New Cat *saved* Tom, the time he got attacked by Miss Matheson's dog. Mr. Tucker was going up and down the road, picking up litter, like he always does, and Tom was with him, holding the trash bag for Mr. Tucker to drop the litter into. And Mr. Tucker was half-way inside a rosebush, trying to reach a packet of pickled onion Monster Munch. And Miss Matheson's dog got out. And it went running at Tom, barking, and baring its teeth. And Tom panicked, and dropped the trash bag, and all the litter spilled out, and he ran off down the road. And Mr. Tucker tried to untangle himself from the bush.

And Miss Matheson's dog chased Tom right down to the bottom of the road, and got him up against Joe-down-the-street's hedge. And, even though Miss Matheson's dog is only the same size as a guinea pig, Tom couldn't get away. Because, for one thing, Tom is only five, and he was born in August, and he's the smallest in his class, and that made Miss Matheson's dog seem much bigger. And, for another thing, Miss Matheson's dog isn't the kind of dog that people say, "Oh, its bark is worse than its

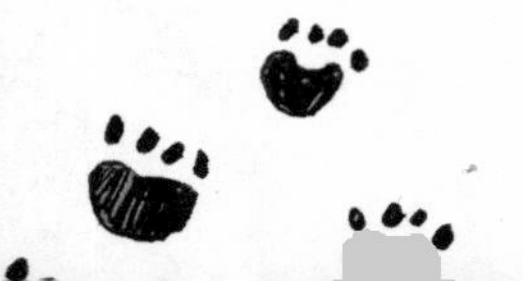

bite" about. It's the opposite kind of dog to that. Because its bark is only a yap. But, like the Milkman said, "Its bite takes you by surprise." And that's why he leaves Miss Matheson's milk on her wall, instead of taking it up to her doorstep.

Anyway, Miss Matheson's dog was jumping up, and baring its teeth, and snapping between Tom's legs. And Mr. Tucker was running down the road, to rescue Tom, when the New Cat came flying over the top of the hedge, hissing, with its ears flat, and its eyes wide, and its fur big. And it swiped

Miss Matheson's dog right between the eyes. And Miss Matheson's dog yelped, and put its head between its paws. And the New Cat held it down on the ground with its claws. And then Miss Matheson came running down the road, in her slippers, with her coal shovel in her hand, and she whacked the New Cat on the head until it let her dog go. And she picked her dog up, and put it under her arm, and kissed it, and said, "What are you doing to my *poor* little Misty?" and took it home.

If Miss Matheson hadn't come out, the New Cat would probably have dragged her dog in dead through the cat flap, like it does with everything else.

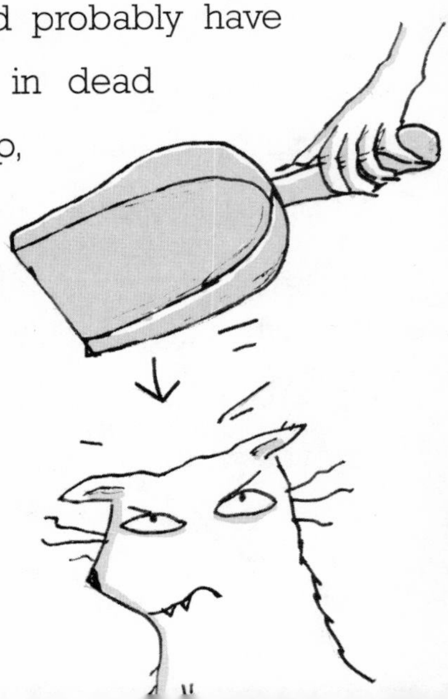

Anyway, after that, Mom called, *"Anna . . . ,"* the way she always does. And she came down the road. And she found me and Tom, and Mr. Tucker (who had leaves and twigs and things stuck in his hair, and a tear in his shirt, and he'd left his blazer behind in the bush), and she said, "Hello" to Mr. Tucker, and Mr. Tucker said, "Hallo" back to Mom.

And then she said, "What have you two been doing to Miss Matheson's dog?"

I said, "Nothing."

And Mom said how it didn't sound like *nothing* to her. Because, she said, "Miss Matheson phoned. And she's *very* upset."

And Miss Matheson had told Mom that me and Tom had been tormenting her dog, and setting the New Cat on it.

Mr. Tucker said, "Unreliable intel, Mrs. Morris. Duff gen. Here's how it went. Dog comes flying out, full pelt, no provocation. Drives Basher downhill till his port engine packs up. Damned thing's got him frozen on the stick, up against the hedge here, going for his goolies, pardon my French. New Cat comes at it, low over the old hedge, and downs bandit with a single burst, bang on target. Then Miss M.'s out. Ten of the best to the New Cat's head. Tears a strip off the sprogs. Your mob not at fault. Wonder old Tommy here hasn't got the twitch."

And then I told Mom what had happened as well. Because sometimes it's hard to understand what Mr. Tucker means, with him being from the War. And Tom said how Miss Matheson's dog had tried to *kill* him, and that the New Cat had *saved his life.*

Mom said, "I think Miss Matheson's dog might be a bit small to kill you, Tom."

Tom said, "It's small, but it's nasty."

And Mr. Tucker said, "I should say it is. Smallness inversely proportionate to its viciousness, Mrs. Morris." And he said the New Cat made a great Rear Gunner.

And Tom said, "It's a *Guard* Cat."

And Mr. Tucker said, "A Guard Cat, Basher, exactly that."

And Tom stuck his chest out. And he gave Mr. Tucker the salute. And Mr. Tucker gave him the salute back.

I wasn't sure if the New Cat was *that* good a Guard Cat. Because, like I told Tom, it attacks things inside the house as well. Like *us*. And our *feet*. And a Guard Cat shouldn't do that, because we are the ones it's meant to guard. The New Cat even attacks Tom, if he hasn't got socks on.

Tom says the New Cat doesn't know that feet belong to *people*. Because whenever it's wet outside, the New Cat stops hunting animals, and comes inside and hunts *us* instead. Sometimes it stands still, *just* inside a door, flat against the wall, and when the door opens, the New Cat flies out from behind it, and throws itself on your feet, and locks on with its claws, and sinks in its teeth. Other times the New Cat goes partway up the stairs, and lies flat, pressing itself against a step, so you can't see it from the top, and when you step down onto the stair it's on, it shoots its paws out and gets you with its claws, and clings on to your ankle.

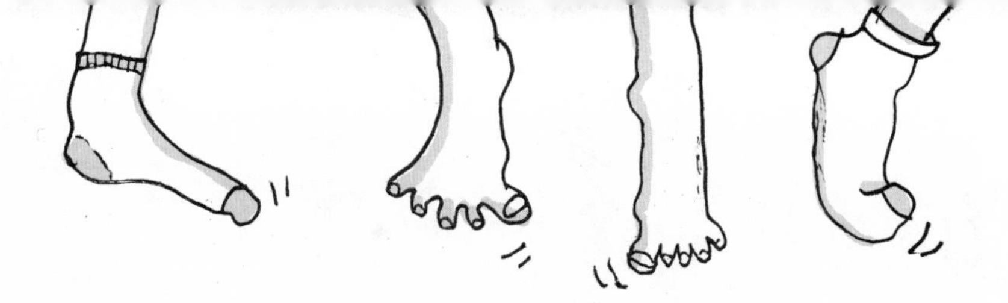

And sometimes the New Cat gets inside the beds, under the covers, right down at the bottom, and waits until you get in to go to sleep. And when you slide your feet down, it pounces, and gets its teeth in, and digs its claws into your toes, trapped under the covers.

And that's why everyone in our house has got scratches, and scabs, and scars on their feet.

And they're always running round in circles screaming, "*Help,* the *New Cat*!" and kicking their legs, to try to shake it off.

And that's why, when the New Cat first went missing, no one, apart from Tom, really cared very much.

CHAPTER 6
The Vicar's Koi Carp

The night before it went missing, the New Cat caught a fish in the Vicarage pond. Not a small fish like Joe-down-the-street once won at the school summer fete. Or a middle-size fish like Mom gets on Friday from the fish-and-chip shop. This was a Really Big Fish. It was the biggest thing the New Cat had ever brought in. And it must have taken ages to catch it, and kill it, and drag it down the road, and get it in through the cat flap.

In the morning there were bits of fish

all over the house. There was a tail on the kitchen table, and scales all up the stairs, and a backbone on the bath mat, and on Tom's pillow, when he woke up, was a big fish head with its eyes wide open.

I wouldn't like it if the New Cat put a fish head in *my* bed, but Tom didn't mind. He shouted out, "Hey, Anna, come and see *this*!"

So I went into Tom's room. And he sat up in bed. And he pointed at his pillow.

"It's a fish head," I said.

Tom said, "Do you think it's a present from the New Cat?"

And I said I thought it probably was. Because I didn't think anyone else would give a present like that.

"The New Cat likes me *best*," Tom said. And he got out of bed, and he picked up the fish head, and he took it into Mom's room, where she was still asleep, and said, *"Look!"*

And he held it near Mom's face.

Mom opened her eyes, and said, "*What the . . . ? Tom*, it's a *fish head*!"

And Tom said, "Yes."

"Where did you *get* it?"

"In my bed."

"Give me *strength,*" Mom said. And she looked at her clock, and then she shot out of bed, because she had overslept. And she grabbed the fish head off Tom, and ran downstairs, and she got the tail off the kitchen table, and put them both in the trash. And then she ran back up, and brushed her teeth, and picked the bones up off the bath mat, and vacuumed the trail of scales all up the stairs.

And she said, "I'm going to Church. . . ."

Because it was Sunday. "If anyone's interested? *Stinking* of *fish*."

Mom didn't used to go to Church much because she only went sometimes to keep Nana company. But after Nana died, when it was her funeral, Mrs. Constantine asked Mom if she could put her name down on the handing-out-the-hymnbook roster. And Mom meant to say "no," but she said "yes" by mistake. And after that she had to go to Church all the time. Because the other people who hand out the hymnbooks were always going away on holiday, and getting mono, and things like that.

When Mom goes to Church, me and Tom go to Sunday School, next door, and do painting and putting on plays instead, and Tom eats all the cookies.

Dad doesn't go to Church. He doesn't even believe in God. He says he believes in staying in bed.

After Church was over, and the Vicar had finished standing by the door, and shaking everyone's hands, and saying, "Go in peace and serve the Lord," he came back inside where Mom was putting the hymnbooks away, and I was waiting, and Tom was collecting up all the cushions for kneeling, and putting them in a big pile by the pulpit (which is the thing the Vicar stands on to speak). And the Vicar said, "Hello," and, "Lovely day," and, "Put the cushions back now, please." And then he asked Tom what we had done in Sunday School.

Tom said how we had eaten cookies.

And the Vicar said, "Anything *else*?"

And Tom shook his head.

And the Vicar said, "I'm sure you *did*. I

know Mrs. Constantine was going to do the story of the loaves and the fishes with you, and make a start on the frieze for the far wall." Which she probably was, but Graham Roberts locked the door when he went to the bathroom, which we're not supposed to do, because he forgot about it again, and he didn't see the big sign that says, DO NOT USE THIS LOCK. IT GETS STUCK!

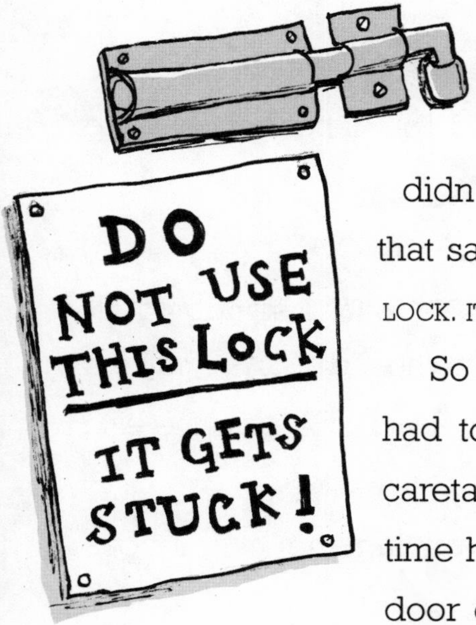

So Mrs. Constantine had to go and get the caretaker, and this time he had to take the door off. And everyone watched. And after that there was only time to do the prayer, and have juice and cookies.

Anyway, the Vicar asked Tom if he knew the story about Jesus and the five loaves, and the two fishes, and how he had fed the five thousand.

And Tom said he didn't.

And the Vicar said how it was from the Gospel according to Saint John, and from Matthew, chapter 14, verses 13 to 21. And he asked Tom if he would like to hear it.

And Tom said, "No thanks."

The Vicar didn't look very pleased. And he breathed in deep, and he did a sigh. And then he did a sniff. And he said, "Can anyone else *smell fish*?"

Mom stopped putting the hymnbooks away.

And the Vicar said, "I've got fish on the brain. Several of mine have gone missing from my pond. There was another one gone this morning when I got up—my best Koi Carp."

Mom didn't say anything. But Tom did. He said, "Mom smells of fish."

The Vicar said, "I'm sure she doesn't."

Tom said, "She does, because the New Cat brought a big fish in through the cat flap and it killed it and put its bits all over the house. And Mom had to clean it up. Its head was on my pillow."

And the Vicar said, "Oh? What did this fish *look* like?"

And Tom said, "Like *this*."

And he held his eyes wide apart and rolled them around and stuck his tongue out.

And the Vicar said, "What color was it?"

And Tom told the Vicar how it was hard to tell what color it was because it was in lots of different bits because its scales were

all up the stairs, and its tail was on the table, and its bones were on the bath mat. And some of it was missing, but its head, which was in his bed, was white and orange with black spots.

And the Vicar said, "That's my best *Koi Carp*! I bought him for breeding. . . ."

And Tom said, "He's in the trash." And then he said, "Are there any more cookies?"

And the Vicar said, "*No.* There *aren't.*" And his neck went all red.

And Mom said, "I am so sorry about your Koi Carp. Can we buy you a replacement?"

The Vicar said, "If you insist."

Which Mom hadn't. Because she only said it once. And if you insist about something, you say it lots of times. Over and over again. Until the other person gives in. But Mom got her purse out of her handbag and said, "How much is it?"

The Vicar said, "Two hundred and twenty pounds."

Mom looked surprised. And then she looked in her purse.

The Vicar said, "I can take a check."

And Mom said, "Oh . . . right . . . yes."

And she got her checkbook out, and wrote "two hundred and twenty pounds" on one. And she gave it to the Vicar. And he put it in his pocket.

When we got home, Dad was still in bed. And me and Tom went in to bounce on it, and wake him up, and Mom came as well, and she told him about the Vicar's Koi Carp, the New Cat, and the check for two hundred and twenty pounds.

Dad said the Vicar would be lucky if there was two hundred and twenty pounds in their bank account. And then he said, "That's *enough bouncing*." And he got out of bed, and started going downstairs to make breakfast, saying things to himself, about the Vicar, and how he should spend less on his pond and more on the poor, like he's always going on about.

The New Cat was halfway up the stairs, lying flat against a step, so Dad couldn't see it, and it probably hadn't had its breakfast either, because when Dad put his foot down onto the stair it was on, the New Cat shot out its paws, and clung on with its claws, and sank in its teeth. And Dad screamed, "Agh, the **NEW CAT!**" And he fell down the rest of the stairs, with the New Cat attached.

When he got to the bottom, he kicked the air until the New Cat came flying off, and hit the wall, and then, while it was still stunned, Dad grabbed the New Cat by the scruff of its neck, and put it out the back door.

And slammed the door shut. And said, **"AND STAY OUT!"** And after that Dad put the lock down on the cat flap.

Tom asked Dad to take the lock off. Because, he said, it wasn't the New Cat's fault, really, about the Vicar's fish. Because cats are *supposed* to catch things. And they don't know how much they cost. And he told

Dad how the New Cat didn't know that feet belonged to people. And how it didn't like it outside. Because it was raining. And that was why it kept running at the cat flap, and banging its head.

But Dad just said, "Tough." And put the bacon under the grill, and cracked the eggs into the frying pan, and turned the radio right up.

And the New Cat put its tail in the air, and walked away down the road.

And Tom watched it through the window.

CHAPTER 7
The Search Party

The New Cat hadn't come back by the time we went to bed.

In the morning, which was Monday, when Tom woke up, he asked, "Has the New Cat come back?"

And Mom said, "No."

And when Tom got home from school, he asked again, "Is the New Cat back?"

And Mom said, "Not yet."

And on Tuesday, and Wednesday, and Thursday, and Friday, Tom asked again about the New Cat, and where it was, and whether it was coming back. And when Saturday came, Tom wouldn't sit with me and have his cereal, in his pajamas, and watch cartoons, or go and meet Suzanne to make plans in the shed. He put his wellies on instead, and went down the road, on his own, and stood at the bottom, and looked up and down.

Mr. Tucker was out picking up litter, and he saw Tom standing at the bottom of the road, and he gave him the salute and called down, "Out early today, Old Chum. Getting a head start on collecting the gravel up, eh?"

Tom shook his head.

"Walking-in-a-straight-line-with-the-old-eyes-closed today, is it?"

Tom shook his head.

"How about plugging away with me at this litter situation, then?"

Tom shook his head again.

So Mr. Tucker went down the road, and he sat on the wall at the bottom, and Tom sat down too. And he said, "Not *woman trouble*, is it, Old Chap?"

And Tom said it wasn't, and he told Mr. Tucker all about what had happened with the New Cat, and the Vicar's fish, and how it had hunted Dad's feet. And how Dad had thrown it out. And locked the cat flap. And how he didn't think it was coming back.

Mr. Tucker said, "Old Rear Gunner missing in action, eh? Black do all round, Basher. Can't have that. What about a recon, eh? Send out a search party, Tom, what do you say?" Tom wiped his nose on his sleeve. And Mr. Tucker got his hankie out, and he held it to Tom's nose, and said, "Give it a good blow." And Tom did. And then he said, "That's the ticket. Now, look tidy. Fling one up."

And Tom stood up straight. And he gave Mr. Tucker the salute. And Mr. Tucker gave him the salute back. And he took Tom down into the village. And they asked everyone they passed if they had seen the New Cat. And no one had. And Mr. Tucker told Tom he thought that the New Cat had probably gone on holiday, or something like that. And it was sure to come back. Because cats were always doing things like that. And he had heard of one cat that went to Spain on a ferry. On its own. By mistake. And it came back in the end. Because, he said, "Thing with cats is, *top-notch navigators*."

After they had been round the village, and asked in all the shops, and bought a bag of sweets, and stopped halfway up the hill for a rest on the

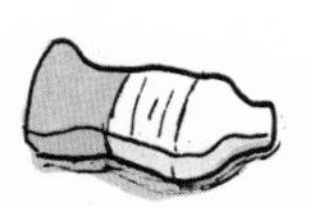

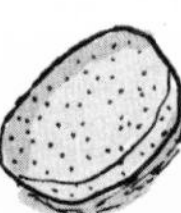

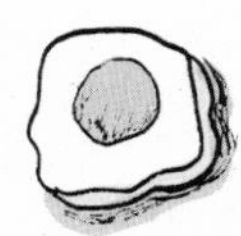
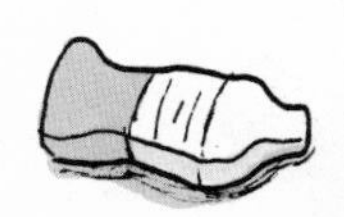

bench—while Mr. Tucker had his puffer, and Tom wet his wellies in the horse trough—they walked back up into our road. Mrs. Tucker came out, and Mr. Tucker said, "Hallo, Tom, look sharp, Squadron Leader."

Mrs. Tucker said, "Hello, Poppet," to Tom, and she said, "*Raymond!* Where have you been?"

And Mr. Tucker said, "Reconnaissance, Dickey. Tom's cat's gone AWOL."

Mrs. Tucker said, "Oh dear, poor old Tom, I'm sorry to hear *that.*"

And then she said, "Raymond, your breakfast is cold, and you're late to take your pills, and in case you've forgotten, your cousins are *still* here."

Mr. Tucker said, "Roger that. T minus two minutes, Dickey."

And he asked Tom, "Where's the rest of your wing? Popsie and so on?" Popsie is what Mr. Tucker calls me. Even though it's not my name. And I've told him I don't like it.

Tom told Mr. Tucker I was in the shed, making plans with Suzanne.

"Old chairborne division, eh?" And he told Mrs. Tucker to take Tom inside and give him a cookie. "Back in a jiffy."

And he went round the side of our house, into the back lane. And he knocked on the shed door.

Me and Suzanne looked through the spy hole, which is a knot of wood at the front of the shed that you can pop in and out.

Suzanne said, "What's the password?"

"Press On Regardless."

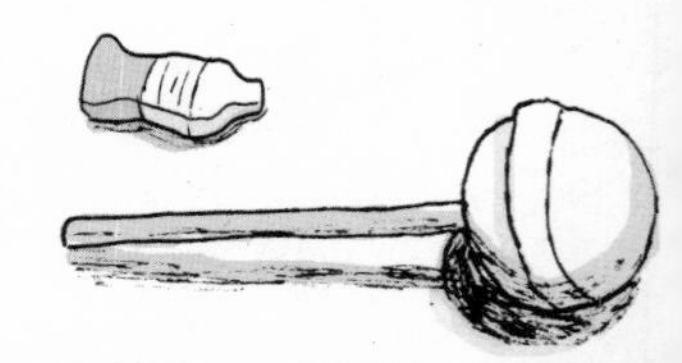

Which it wasn't. But we opened the door anyway because Mr. Tucker had never knocked on the shed before so it was probably important. He came inside, and he looked at the wasp trap, and the worm box, and he tried to look at the plan that me and Suzanne were working on. Which we hadn't got very far with because we had only done the title, which was too long, and took up most of the piece of paper. It said:

Anna's And Suzanne's Plan To Find Out If There Are Holes In All The Walls In All The Lofts In All The Houses In The Road And, If There Are, Whether We Can Climb Through Them And Come Out In The House At The Bottom, Which Is Joe-Down-The-Street's.

I rolled the plan up so Mr. Tucker couldn't see it.

Mr. Tucker said, "Look here, I can see you bods are hard up against it with your bumph and all that, but this briefing comes down from Brass Hats, so look lively; simple enough op for your division, Popsie. As of eleven hundred hours, we want all personnel assisting Basher with this damned Cat Situation. Went AWOL on Sunday, of course, and so far it's still Missing In Action. Don't like to mention moral fiber, or the lack of, but it doesn't do to leave a chap's cat unaccounted for, so fingers out for you and Blondie on this one, eh, Popsie, what do you say?"

I said, "Okay."

And Mr. Tucker said, "That's the ticket. Best of British. Your group's got the green, Popsie, chocks away."

And he gave the salute. And Suzanne gave him the salute back. But I didn't, because the last time I gave Mr. Tucker the salute, which was ages ago, when I was about eight, Mr. Tucker said I didn't do it right, and he made me do it again, about a million times, and he kept saying, "More power on the up." And also because I didn't really *want* to try to find the New Cat, because I wanted to do the plan for the loft and the holes, and climbing through all the houses in the road, and coming out at the bottom in Joe-down-the-street's.

Tom came to the shed with the cookies from Mrs. Tucker.

And Mr. Tucker said, "Right-o. Relatives now, Basher. Black do all round."

And he messed Tom's hair up. And then he went home.

When he was gone, Suzanne said how she didn't know why Mr. Tucker called her "Blondie" when her hair was brown. And she said, "I don't know why he says that it's *your* division, and *your* group, either, because it's not like you're in charge." Which is true. Because normally Suzanne is. Especially when it comes to investigations. Because Suzanne knows everything about stuff like that, because her Mom lets her watch all the police dramas on TV, and one of her uncles is a Special Constable, and she's got a book from the Brownie Jumble sale called, *Private Detective: A Practical Handbook*. Which she keeps under her bed. And she's read it a billion times.

Suzanne said, "You didn't tell me the New Cat was missing."

Which was true, because I forgot. And because I didn't really care about the New Cat. Not until Tom came into the shed, after Mr. Tucker left, and his eyes were all red, and his T-shirt was wet, and he was chewing his coat sleeve like he sometimes does when he's upset.

And he said, "Are you making a plan for finding the New Cat?"

And then I said, "Yes." And so did Suzanne.

And Tom stopped chewing his sleeve, and he sat down and started eating his cookies.

And Suzanne put the plan for the loft and the holes behind the stepladders, under the shelf with the wasp trap on it and the worm collection. And I got my dictionary, and I looked up "AWOL." Because that's what Mr. Tucker said the New Cat was.

And this is what it said:

AWOL [A.W.O.L.] ✦ *noun*
Absent With Out Leave (A.W.O.L.) normally used about a soldier or other military person who is absent from duty without permission, but without the intention of deserting

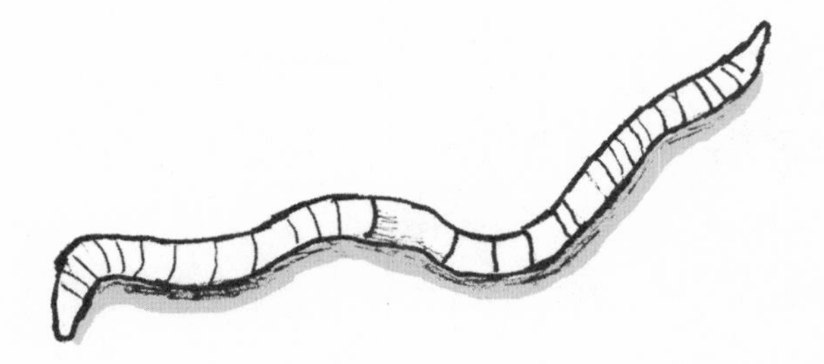

CHAPTER 8

What Might Have Happened to the New Cat

Anna's And Suzanne's And Tom's List Of All The Things That Might Have Happened To The New Cat

1. Killed
   (By A Dog Or Wolves Or Bears Or A Car)
2. Gone Off In A Huff
3. Gone Hunting
4. Gone On Holiday

The first thing on the list was "Killed." I didn't think a dog would be able to kill the New Cat because we had never met one that it was even scared of. And Tom agreed, because, he said, "In a fight with a dog, the New Cat would win. But," he said, "it might not win against wolves or bears. Especially if they were hungry, or in a big pack."

You don't really get packs of wolves or bears round here, but I put it on the list anyway because Tom's eyes were still pink and he had finished all his cookies.

I said maybe the New Cat had been hit by a car. Like happened to our *Old* Cat, in the back lane, when Miss Matheson ran it over.

But Suzanne said she

didn't think Miss Matheson *had* run over the *New* Cat, because when she ran the Old Cat over, Suzanne found cat blood on Miss Matheson's car tires. And there wasn't any blood on them this time, because Suzanne went out and checked. And anyway, like Tom said, we didn't *just* find cat blood when the Old Cat got run over. Because we also found the Old Cat, squashed flat, out the back, by Miss Matheson's gate. And no one had found the New Cat squashed flat anywhere.

So we crossed number 1, "**Killed (By A Dog Or Wolves Or Bears Or A Car),**" off.

Number 2 on the list was "**Gone Off In A Huff.**" Which was Suzanne's idea. Suzanne goes off in huffs, if you do something she doesn't like, and then you have to wait for ages, and try and find her, and say sorry, and all that. But the New Cat doesn't go in for huffs much, because it's not the sort of cat that wants people coming after it. You can't even touch it without gardening gloves on. And, anyway, the New Cat had been gone for nearly a week. And even Suzanne has never stayed in a huff *that* long. But Suzanne said that she would, if she had been thrown out, and it was raining, and she kept banging her head on the cat flap.

So we went up and down the road, looking for the New Cat, and we put bits of ham out, and banged on a saucer of milk with a spoon, and shouted, "Puss, puss, puss, puss, puss." Like Nana sometimes did, before she died, to get the Old Cat to come in at night. But the New Cat didn't come. So we crossed "**Huff**" off the list as well.

The next thing was "**Gone Hunting.**"

Because, like Suzanne said, "The New Cat is always off killing things. And maybe it has had to go farther to find some, because it has already killed all the things in the garden, and there probably wasn't anything left alive, nearby."

But Tom told Suzanne how the New Cat always brings the things it has hunted back, to hide them in the house. And how it doesn't go hunting when it's wet outside. Because that's when it stays in, and sleeps, and hunts feet in the house. And it had been raining all week. So we crossed "Gone Hunting" off too.

Tom said the New Cat might have "Gone On Holiday," like Mr. Tucker said. And he told us about the cat that went to Spain on the ferry by itself, by mistake, and found its way back. Suzanne said she didn't think cats went on holiday on their own,

even if it wasn't on purpose, because she thought that was only the kind of thing that grown-ups say to shut you up and stop you getting upset. So we went into the house and put "cat, Spain, holiday, mistake" into the computer. And what Mr. Tucker said was true. Because there was a picture of the cat, and it had got in the news. And it said:

Missing Cat Found on Ferry

Stowaway Sandi was discovered by stunned ferry staff under a truck on the P&O Pride of Bilbao, which had traveled all the way from Portsmouth. The ferry crew took the tom to a vet, who was able to tell from an embedded microchip where he was from. Sandi had a luxurious return trip, fed on a special menu of fresh salmon, grilled chicken, and milk in an en-suite cabin with a sea view.

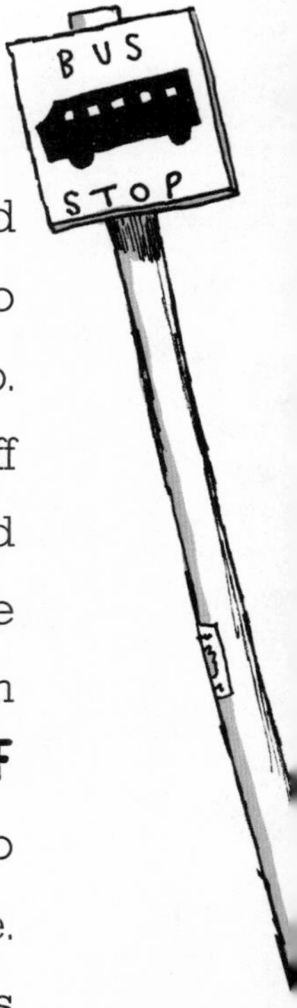

But the New Cat didn't have an embedded microchip. It didn't even have a collar, so no one would know where to bring it back to. And, like Suzanne said, it could have got off the boat in Spain, or something like that. And we couldn't go there to look for it, because Suzanne isn't even allowed past the bottom bus stop because her Dad says it's **"OUT OF BOUNDS."** And that meant all we could do was wait, to see if the New Cat came home. Which wasn't much of a plan. And that was all the things on our list.

So I said, "Let's go and see Mrs. Rotherham." And Suzanne said that was a good idea, because of how Mrs. Rotherham used to be in the police so she knows about these kinds of things. And Tom said it was a good idea too. Because Mrs. Rotherham always has cookies.

CHAPTER 9
The Suspect List

We told Mrs. Rotherham all about what had happened with the New Cat and the Vicar's Koi Carp and how Dad had thrown it out and locked the cat flap, and how it still hadn't come back. And Mrs. Rotherham went and made some tea, and Tom asked if she had any cookies, and she brought out the tin, and she said, "When I was in the police," which was probably about a million years ago, "the first thing we did when a person went missing was to fill out a *Missing Person Alert* form." And she went inside her cupboard. And she found a form. And she brought it out. And she crossed "Person" out, and put "Pet" instead. And me and Tom and Suzanne sat by the fire and drank the tea and ate the cookies and filled it in. And when it was finished, the Missing Pet Alert Form looked like this:

Missing ~~Person~~ PET Alert

SURNAME: Cat

FORENAME: The New

DOB (Mrs. Rotherham said this means Date of Birth): Unknown

PHYSICAL DESCRIPTION: small, angry animal with four legs and a tail

HEIGHT: About up to Tom's new bruise

BUILD: scrawny

HAIR, COLOR AND STYLE: Gray, matted

EYE COLOR: Green

CLOTHING: None
(it used to have a flea collar, but it chewed it off)
ANY DISTINGUISHING FEATURES:
A tooth that hangs down over its mouth
KNOWN RISKS: Hunts most things, especially birds, mice, moles, voles, rats, rabbits, spiders, wasps, flies, and feet
ADDITIONAL INFORMATION: Do not approach without gardening gloves
CONTACT DETAILS: Anna and Tom Morris,
Number 5, Spoutwell Lane

Mrs. Rotherham looked at the form and said she thought it was very good.

Suzanne asked, "What did you do after that?"

"I'd ask myself, has this person gone somewhere of their own accord, or are we dealing with something altogether more untoward? Then I'd do some poking about the place. More often than not, if there's a suspect, it'll be someone very close to the person who's missing. A neighbor, maybe. A family member, more often than not. And then it's motive, of course, and whether or not the suspect had an opportunity, and are there any prior convictions?"

Suzanne wrote down everything that Mrs. Rotherham said in the notepad.

"After that, it's a rather less interesting business. Putting up 'Missing' posters, talking to passersby, handing out fliers. Offer a reward."

We finished our tea. And Tom ate the last cookie. And Suzanne finished writing, and put the notepad in her pocket. And we said "thank you" to Mrs. Rotherham. And went back down the road.

When we got back to the shed, Suzanne wrote on the top of a piece of paper, People Who Might Have Taken The New Cat, and she underlined it.

I said I couldn't think of anyone who would take the New Cat. Because it wasn't the sort of cat that people would want. Because before it went missing, *we* didn't even want it ourselves.

Tom said, "Someone might take it to make a fur coat, like Cruella de Vil does in *101 Dalmatians*."

But I didn't think *anyone* would wear the *New Cat's* coat. Even if it was washed, and had conditioner put on it, and was given a blow-dry. Because the New Cat's coat isn't very nice, and it's got lots of bits missing from all the times it's been in fights.

Suzanne said, "There might be another reason why someone would take it."

And I said, "Like what?"

And Suzanne said, "*Revenge.*" And then she wrote on the paper:

1. The Vicar, for killing his Koi Carp
2. Miss Matheson, for attacking her dog
3. Anna's Dad, for costing £220 to buy the Vicar a new fish

I thought Suzanne might be right about the Vicar and Miss Matheson, but I didn't think Dad really wanted revenge much, because all he ever wants is to watch football, and drink beer, and he probably couldn't be bothered to kidnap the New Cat.

But Suzanne looked in the notepad, at all the things Mrs. Rotherham had said, and she read, *"More often than not it's a family member."* And she wrote, Motive? Yes. Opportunity? Yes. And then she said, "Has your Dad got any prior convictions?"

And I said, "I don't know."

And Suzanne wrote, Possible prior convictions. And she underlined Anna's Dad. And she put the notepad in her pocket, and she got the binoculars, and she said, "Let's go to the Vicarage."

And Tom asked us to wait while he went inside, and got his swimming goggles, even though, like Suzanne said, "You won't really need them."

And we went up the road.

CHAPTER 10
Poking About the Place

Suzanne looked through the Vicarage gate with the binoculars. And then I looked as well. And then Tom. But none of us could see the New Cat, especially not Tom because he had his goggles on, and the binoculars backward. And then we opened the gate and went in because, like I told Suzanne, it was a Saturday, so the Vicar would be doing weddings.

We held the binoculars up to the letter box, and up to all the windows at the front of the house. And then me and Suzanne went round the back. And Tom stayed at the front, behind the hedge, to keep watch.

Me and Suzanne looked through the binoculars into all the windows at the back. And we couldn't see the New Cat there, either.

Suzanne said, "The New Cat isn't the sort of animal that someone could take easily." Which was true. "Which means there was probably a fight. So if the Vicar took it, we should see signs of a struggle."

So we went all round the Vicarage looking for some. But we didn't find any. And, after a while, Suzanne said, "The New Cat isn't here." So we went back round to the front.

When we got there, Tom wasn't standing behind the hedge, looking out. He was lying on the ground, with his face in the fishpond.

"Tom?!" I said. "What are you doing?"

Tom lifted his head up. "I'm looking for the New Cat, in case the Vicar has drowned it." And he put his face back in the water, and blew out, so bubbles came up, like he learned at swimming club. And then his head came up again, and he said, "It's not here." And he wiped his goggles with his sleeve, and his tongue as well, because, he said, "I forgot to close my mouth," and it had quite a lot of green slime on it.

And then we went down the road, and round the back, to Miss Matheson's.

We got down on the ground in the back lane beside Miss Matheson's fence, and looked through the binoculars.

I said if she *had* taken the New Cat, I didn't think Miss Matheson would keep it in the garden. Because, for one thing, it would be too easy for it to escape. And, for another thing, someone might spot it. And, for an even other thing, it might attack Miss Matheson's dog.

And Tom said he didn't think Miss Matheson would keep the New Cat in her house, either, because it would hunt her feet, and tear up her furniture, and it might attack her dog there as well.

And Suzanne said that she thought we were right, and if Miss Matheson was going to keep the New Cat anywhere, it would have to be in her garage, and it would probably be tied up.

So me and Suzanne and Tom climbed over the gate, and we crept over the gravel, and ran over to the garage, and I gave Suzanne a boost up, and she looked in through the garage window. And then we swapped around.

Miss Matheson's garage was very neat. There were rakes and brooms and hoes all

in a line. And plant pots in order of size. And one shelf for jars, and another for paint, and one for string and twine. But there wasn't any sign of the New Cat anywhere.

"It's not here," I said.

I got down from the garage window. And we started walking back toward the gate. And when we were halfway across we stopped, because we heard someone say, "Ahem."

Miss Matheson was standing on the other side of the gate. In the back lane. With her arms crossed. Watching us. And Mom was standing beside her.

Miss Matheson said, "This is the kind of thing I'm talking about, Mrs. Morris." And she said how she wasn't the only one on the street who was upset with our family, and our pets. Because she had spoken to the Vicar, and he had told her about our cat, and what it had done to his Koi Carp. And she had seen us all in his garden, just now, meddling in his pond.

And Mom said, "*Anna*, is that true?"

And I said, "No."

And Mom said, "Why has Tom got goggles on? And what's that green slime?" And Mom took me and Tom and Suzanne inside.

And Miss Matheson called, "If it happens once more, I shall call the *police*."

Suzanne said that we could call the police on Miss Matheson, actually, because of her dog, and how it attacked Tom. Because, she said, "Miss Matheson's dog should wear a muzzle." Which Suzanne knows all about from when her cousin went to court.

Mom said she was pretty sure Miss Matheson's dog wasn't covered by the Dangerous Dogs Act, because it was a Chihuahua, and they didn't have to have muzzles on. And then she said, "And in any case, Suzanne, that's not the point."

And Tom said, "What does 'the point' mean?"

And Mom said, "It means you had no business going in her garden, and looking into her garage. Or the Vicar's. What were you doing?"

I didn't say anything and nor did Suzanne. Tom said, "The Vicar and Miss Matheson have taken the New Cat, and drowned it and tied it up and things like that."

And Mom said, "No one has taken the New Cat, Tom."

And she said me and Suzanne had to stop filling Tom's head with rubbish. Because it wasn't fair, and it wasn't funny.

And I said how it wasn't meant to be funny because, I said, "It's very serious. And that's why me and Suzanne and Tom are trying to find it."

Mom said, "If someone's got the New Cat, it's more likely to have been *adopted* than *abducted.*"

I got my dictionary and looked "adopted" up. This is what it said:

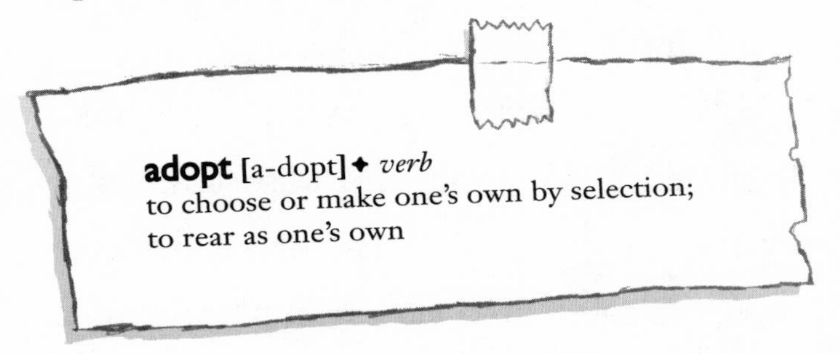

adopt [a-dopt] ✦ *verb*
to choose or make one's own by selection; to rear as one's own

And this is what it said about "abducted":

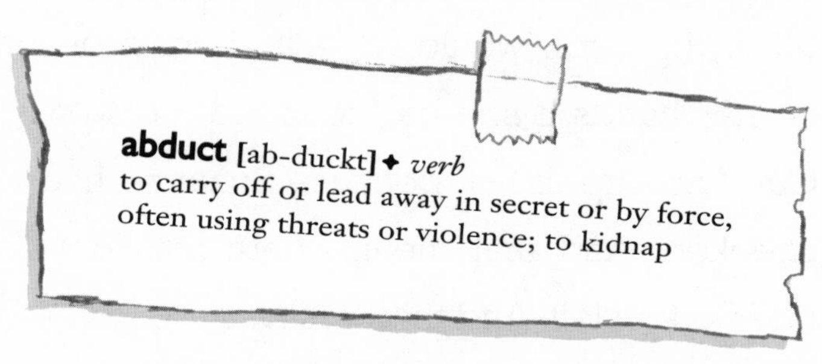

But whether the New Cat had been abducted or adopted didn't make much difference, I didn't think. Because you can't just go round adopting pets that already belong to other people.

Because, I said, "Imagine if someone just came and adopted me or Tom?"

Mom said, "Ha. *Imagine!*"

And she told us we had to play inside for a while.

And Suzanne got the notepad out and crossed the Vicar and Miss Matheson off the list because, like she said, we had done a search, and we hadn't seen the New Cat, and there weren't any signs of a struggle. And Miss Matheson would have had scratches on her hands if she had touched the New Cat. And she didn't, because Suzanne had checked. And that meant there was only one person left. And that was *Dad.*

"Let's interrogate him," Suzanne said.

This is what my dictionary says "interrogate" means:

interrogate [in-ter-o-gate] ✦ *verb*
to ask someone a lot of questions for a long time in order to get information, sometimes using threats or violence

Suzanne said, "We need to do a lie detector test."

Because, she said, her book tells you all about how when people tell lies, their eyes look up, and off to the left, and they touch their mouth with their hand.

So she said, "We'll ask him all about the New Cat, and what has happened to it. And the lie detector test will say if he's telling the truth."

Dad was watching football with his hands over his eyes.

I told him how we were trying to find out what had happened to the New Cat.

Dad said, "Uh-huh." Like he does when he isn't listening.

So I said how it was very important and we needed to ask him some questions.

And Dad said, "Yup."

And I said, "Now."

And Dad said, "Yeah, yeah." And then he said, "At halftime."

And Suzanne said, "Or we could go and tell your Mom about the loft, Anna, and how all the broken things from under the stairs are up there."

And then Dad jumped up, out of his chair, and said, "No, no, don't do that! I'll answer your questions."

And Suzanne said, "I thought so." And she turned the TV off. And she told Dad to turn his chair around. And she closed the curtains. And she turned on the lamp, and she pointed it at Dad. And she walked around the room.

And she whispered to me to ask Dad a question I knew he would lie to, so I said, "Do you like going on long walks with Suzanne's Dad?"

And Dad said, "Urm, yes, I do." And he touched his mouth and his eyes went up to the left. And Suzanne said, "That's a *lie*! Ask him again."

So I said, "I'm going to ask you again. Do you like going on walks with Suzanne's Dad?"

And Dad said, "Urm, well, no, not that much." And he didn't put his hand on his mouth, or move his eyes. So we knew that the lie detector test was working.

And after that Suzanne asked Dad lots of questions really fast, close to his face, like, "Do you like the New Cat?" and, "Are you glad it's gone?" and, "Do you hope it never comes back?"

And Dad said, "Urm, no, yes, I do, I'm sorry, Tom."

And Suzanne said, "And that's why you took it and tied it up, or killed it, isn't it?"

And Dad said, "What? Oh, yes, of course, that's *exactly* it." But his hand touched his mouth, and his eyes went up, and to the left, which meant he was lying.

And then Tom went very close up to Dad, with the lamp, and he pointed it right in his face, and Dad said, "*Ah*, I'm *blind*."

And Tom said, "Have you kidnapped the New Cat, Dad?" And he looked right in his eyes.

And Dad said, "No, Tom, of course not." And it wasn't a lie because he looked straight back at Tom and his hand didn't touch his mouth.

So Suzanne said, "No further questions."

And she opened the curtains, and turned the lamp off, and put the TV back on, and Dad turned his chair around and started watching the football again.

And me and Tom and Suzanne went back to the shed and looked in the notepad for what Mrs. Rotherham said to do next.

CHAPTER 11

Missing

The next thing after "poking about to see if it's a neighbor or a family member" was to put up "Missing" posters and hand out fliers and offer a reward.

So Suzanne drew two pictures of the New Cat, one big one for the poster and a smaller one for the flier. And Tom started coloring them in.

And then Suzanne had to draw the big one again, because Tom put green stripes on the New Cat's body, and gave it red feet, which, like Suzanne said, was nice, but wasn't exactly what the New Cat looked like.

And she told Tom to color the New Cat in gray, so people would know what cat it was. And when the pictures were finished, I put the words on.

This is what the poster looked like:

And the flier was like this:

And then we all went to see how much money we had for the reward.

Suzanne asked her Dad for her pocket money, which is meant to be three pounds fifty, but after Suzanne's fines for not eating her onions, and for losing her shoes, and not coming home straight from school, it was only eighty-five pence.

I had already had my pocket money, and

next week's. I asked Mom if I could have the week after next's as well, but she said, "No, you can't. You do this every week. When it's spent it's spent." I checked in my pocket to see if I had any left. There was only £1.49.

Tom said he had lots of money. Which he always does. Because he doesn't have anything to spend it on so it just adds up. He brought his piggy bank out to the shed, and we opened it up. And tipped the money out on the table. And I counted it. And Suzanne said she didn't think I had counted it right. So I said, "You count it then." And she did. Out loud, and when she was finished, she did it again, to check. And she took ages. And said every sum out loud. And I undid my shoes and did them back up again, because I was sick of hearing sums. Because I don't like them in school, and I especially don't like doing them on a Saturday, in the shed, when it isn't time for math because it's supposed to be time for finding out who took the New Cat.

Suzanne put the amount for the reward on the bottom of the poster, and the flier, which was £26.79. And then we started to make more. Suzanne drew another outline of the New Cat, a big one for the poster and small for the flier, and Tom started coloring them in, and I had to keep an eye on him so he didn't do it green stripes with red feet again. And I wrote the words. And put the reward amount on the bottom of each one. It was already starting to get dark, and we had only finished two posters. "If we had a photocopier, we could make as many as we liked," I said. There's a photocopier in Suzanne's house.

Suzanne said, "No, we're not using it." Because last time, when we tried to

photocopy her Dad's dictionary, because he wouldn't let us borrow it, Suzanne's Dad went mad about us using all the paper. And the ink. And because the photocopier overheated. And he said, **"THE DICTIONARY IS TWENTY-ONE THOUSAND THREE HUNDRED AND FORTY-THREE PAGES LONG, FOR CRYING OUT LOUD, SUZANNE!"** And he had to get a man to come out and fix it.

"There's a photocopier in the cottage at the Church," Tom said. Which was true. And it was Sunday the next day.

So Suzanne said that in the morning we should all get up early, and go to Sunday School, to use it. And afterward we could put loads of posters up, and hand fliers out, all around the village.

And then we heard Suzanne's Dad in the back lane, saying,

"SUZANNE, YOU'RE LATE. I WANT FIFTY PENCE OF THAT POCKET MONEY BACK!" And Suzanne took it out of the reward money on the table. And changed the amount on the poster and the flier. And then she went home.

CHAPTER 12
Cats

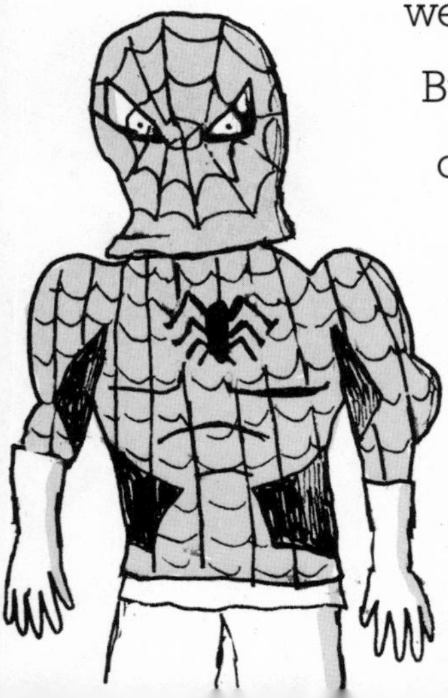

I set my alarm, and in the morning, when it went off, I went into Tom's room and woke him up. Tom got out of bed and put his Spider-Man suit on, with the built-in muscles. I wasn't sure if you're allowed to wear a Spider-Man suit in Church. But Tom said he would put his coat on top, and wear his smart shoes, and leave the mask behind. So I said it was all right. Because once Tom has decided what

he's wearing, it's hard to make him change his mind. Unless you pin him down. Like Dad had to, for a wedding, when Tom was meant to be a page boy and he refused to take his frog wellies off.

Me and Tom had our cereal, and brushed our teeth. And when we were ready, we went in to see Mom, who was still in bed.

Mom said, "Why are you up?"

"For Sunday School," I said.

Mom said she wasn't going to Church because it wasn't her turn for handing out the hymnbooks and she'd gone off it since everything with the Vicar and his Koi Carp.

I asked if me and Tom could go on our own, since we were ready. Mom looked at the clock and said, "You're going to be very early."

So I said we would probably just sit and read the Bible, with Mrs. Constantine, until everyone arrived.

Mom looked at me a bit strange, with her eyebrows up, like she does sometimes. And she shook her head, and said, "Fine." And she asked Tom, "Are you going dressed as Spider-Man?"

Tom said how he wasn't because he was going to put his coat on top, and his smart shoes, and he was leaving his mask behind.

And me and Tom said good-bye, and went out to the shed, and got the poster and the flier. And then we went next door to call on Suzanne.

We rang three times, and Suzanne's Dad opened the window really fast, and leaned out in his dressing gown, and shouted, **"YES? IS THERE A FIRE? IT'S SUNDAY MORNING, FOR CRYING OUT LOUD!"**

Mrs. Constantine said it was nice to see Suzanne at Sunday School, because she doesn't normally come. And she asked what Suzanne would like to do.

And Suzanne said that she would like to use the photocopier.

And Mrs. Constantine said, "Oh."

And Suzanne showed Mrs. Constantine the "Missing" poster and the flier about the New Cat.

Mrs. Constantine said that the photocopier was only supposed to be used for things that were to do with the Church, like the parish magazine, and hymn sheets, and community things.

Suzanne said, "The New Cat was in the community. Before it went missing."

And then Graham Roberts came in, and he said that he had seen the Vicar use the photocopier to copy a magazine, called *Pond Construction and Koi Carp Keeping*. And that wasn't to do with the Church. And then he said that he could show us how to use the photocopier, if we liked, because he had used it before, to photocopy his dog, before it died. And he brought a piece of paper out of his pocket, which was all crumpled, that had the photocopied dog on it. And he showed it to Mrs. Constantine.

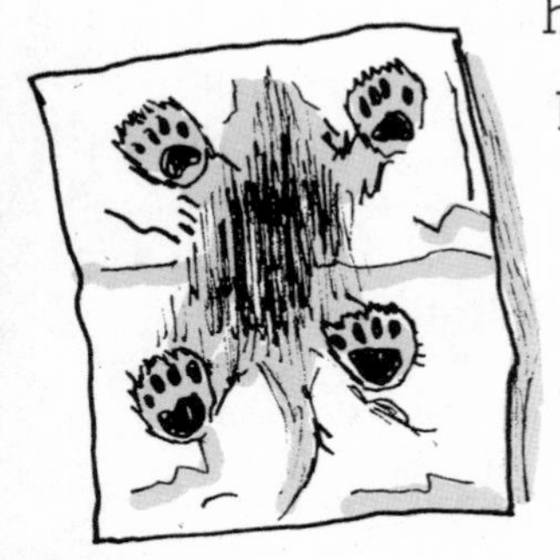

You couldn't see much, apart from the pads on the dog's paws. And a bit of fur. Mrs. Constantine said, "All right, fine, but don't use all the paper. And if anyone needs the toilet today, you'll just have to whistle so we know you're in there, because we're still without a door until the caretaker can put it back on."

So me and Tom and Suzanne and Graham Roberts went upstairs to the room where the photocopier is, where all the old hymnbooks are, and the cloths for the altar, and the gold crosses. And Graham switched the photocopier on. And Suzanne gave him the poster, and the flier.

And Graham looked at them, and then he said, "Emma Hendry has lost her cat as well. That's why she was upset at school on Friday. And that's why Mrs. Peters said I should say sorry, even though I hadn't done anything, except paint her hair by mistake."

Suzanne said, "Joe-down-the-street's babysitter Brian has lost his cat too." And she said, "So that's three cats that have vanished."

And Graham said, "There could be more."

And Suzanne said, "Yes." Because, she

said, "Those are only the ones we know about."

And Graham said, "It's probably a *conspiracy*." And he started the machine. And then he said, "Have you ever heard of the Cat Lady?"

And Tom said he had, because he said, "She's in *Batman*, and Batman is one of my favorites, after Spider-Man, and Bob the Builder."

Graham Roberts said, "That's *Catwoman*. She has cat ears, and a tail, and black boots. This is the *Cat Lady*. She doesn't look like that. She wears a blanket, and when it's raining she puts a carrier bag on her head, and she never has any shoes on."

Tom said how he hadn't heard of the Cat Lady in that case. And neither had me or Suzanne.

Graham said, "It's probably her who is kidnapping the cats." And he said he would show us where her house was, if we liked, after Church.

Suzanne said she wasn't sure, because we would be busy handing out fliers, and putting posters up, and all that. And because, like she told Tom afterward, Graham sometimes tells lies, like the time it was Emma Hendry's turn to talk about "Something I Like," on the carpet, in Mrs. Peters's class, and she did it all about unicorns. Afterward Graham told Emma that his Gran had a unicorn, on her farm, and Emma could come for dinner, and see it, if she liked. And, after she went, Emma said that Graham's Gran's unicorn was only an old Shetland pony that had an ice-cream cone tied on its head, on a piece of elastic.

Graham said, "The Cat Lady's house is

only in the marketplace. You can see it from the Church gate."

So we said we would go. And the photocopier was finished, so we took the posters and fliers, and went back downstairs.

Mrs. Constantine said it was time for the prayer.

Tom asked if she would put the New Cat in it. And Mrs. Constantine said she would.

And then she said, "Right, eyes closed, hands together."

And she did the prayer, which went,

Dear God most high, hear and bless
Thy beasts and singing birds:
And guard with tenderness
Small things that have no words.

And then she said, "And please take care of the New Cat, which is missing."

And Graham Roberts said, "It's been kidnapped by the Cat Lady."

And Mrs. Constantine said, "Right . . ."

And Graham Roberts said, "You can ask my Gran, because she knows all about her and she doesn't tell lies."

And Mrs. Constantine said, "Amen." Which means, "So be it," and, "That's the end," and also, like Tom says, "It's time for cookies." And Tom ate about ten. Until Mrs. Constantine took the tin from him. And then we all went into Church for the last bit at the end. And the Vicar was saying, "Ye have heard that it hath been said, an eye for an eye, and a tooth for a tooth: But I say unto you, that ye resist not evil: but whosoever shall smite thee on thy right cheek, turn to him the other also."

And Suzanne whispered, "See, Anna, *revenge*."

When Church was finished, the Vicar went and stood outside, by the door. And when all the people came out, he shook their hands, and asked if he would be seeing them at Evensong, and told them to "Go in peace and serve the Lord."

And then me and Tom and Suzanne gave each person a flier, and said, "And look out for the New Cat."

When everyone was gone, Graham Roberts said, "Follow me," and we went over to the Church gate. And we looked through it. And Graham pointed to a big house, on the other side of the marketplace, and he said, "*That* is where the Cat Lady lives."

And then he went home.

Me and Tom and Suzanne stood and looked at the house. Suzanne said, "It doesn't look like anyone lives in it." Which it

didn't. Because all the paint on the front was cracking, and peeling off. And two of the windows were broken, and one had cardboard in it, instead of glass. And there were lots of tiles missing from the roof. And there was a bird's nest at the top of the drainpipe. And the chimney looked like it might fall off. And there were dead plants in the window boxes.

We crossed the marketplace to look at it close up. Next to the door was a big window, like you get in a shop. The window was so dirty you could hardly see through it.

I wiped it with my sleeve, but it didn't make much difference because most of the dirt was on the inside. Behind the window, a little way back, was an old net curtain, which had gone all greasy and gray. And, in front of the curtain, on the window ledge, there were three fruit boxes, like you get from the greengrocers. And inside each box was a dirty old blanket. And on top of each blanket was a cat. Beside the cats there was a sign. I breathed on the window and wiped it again, and tried to read what the sign said. "These . . . cats . . . are not . . . forced to sit . . . here. They do so of their own . . . free . . . will. . . ."

Me and Tom and Suzanne looked at one another. And then we looked back at the sign.

Suzanne said, "If nobody lives here, who wrote the sign?"

And Tom said, "And who looks after the cats?"

And I said, "Maybe Graham Roberts is right about the Cat Lady. And the Kidnapping. And the Conspiracy."

We pressed our faces against the window.

"Let's put the posters up and go home," I said.

But we stayed, looking. Then the curtain twitched, and I saw two hands, pulling it apart, and in the gap, above them, there was a face, with a blanket round it, and it looked out, and its eyes were wide, and its mouth was open.

I screamed. And the face in the window screamed back.

And I dropped all the posters and fliers.

And Suzanne said, **"RUN!"** And we did.

And we didn't stop until we got to the shed.

CHAPTER 13

The Stakeout

We locked the shed door. And stood against it. And we stayed very quiet.

After ages, Suzanne popped out the little knot of wood in the spy hole. And looked through.

Tom was jumping from foot to foot, like he does when he gets excited. And then, if he doesn't get to the toilet quick, he wets himself and gets upset.

"Do you need to pee?" I said. Tom

nodded his head. He reached for the door.

"Don't open it," I said. "Can't you go in the shed?" I looked around for something.

"No!" said Suzanne. "He can't." And she got the binoculars down from the shelf and opened the door a crack, and looked up and down the road. "Quick. Just go there, on Miss Matheson's side."

Tom's not really allowed to pee outside because last time he did it, when Mom saw him, from in the kitchen, she tapped on the window, and said, "*Oi*, do you *mind*? Those are my herbs. We don't want your pee in our shepherd's pie." But he didn't look like he would make it into the house. So I held the shed door open, and kept watch, just in case the person whose face we saw in the window had followed us.

Once Tom was back inside, and I'd locked the door again, Suzanne started writing on a piece of paper:

Whose was the face in the window?

Was it the Cat Lady?

Has she got the New Cat?

And she said, "These are the things that we need to find out."

"How?" I asked.

And Suzanne said, "We'll have to go back to the house. Who's going to come?"

I said, "Urm . . ."

Tom said, "I am."

So I said I would too. "But only to look, from far away, like in the Churchyard, through the gate, or from behind the stone cross in the marketplace, through the binoculars."

Suzanne said, "It will be a Stakeout." And she wrote, Anna's and Suzanne's And Tom's

Plan to steak out the Cat Lady's House on the top of a piece of paper. And she said how detectives do "steak outs" all the time.

I looked "steak out" up in my dictionary, which wasn't easy. And, when I found it, this is what it said:

stakeout [steyk-owt] ✦ *noun*
the surveillance of a location by the police, as in anticipation of a crime or the arrival of a wanted person

And then we looked in Suzanne's dictionary as well. And it said:

stakeout [steyk-owt] ✦ *noun informal*
a period of secret surveillance of a building or an area by police in order to observe someone's activities

And Suzanne said that after we had done the stakeout, we would probably have to do a

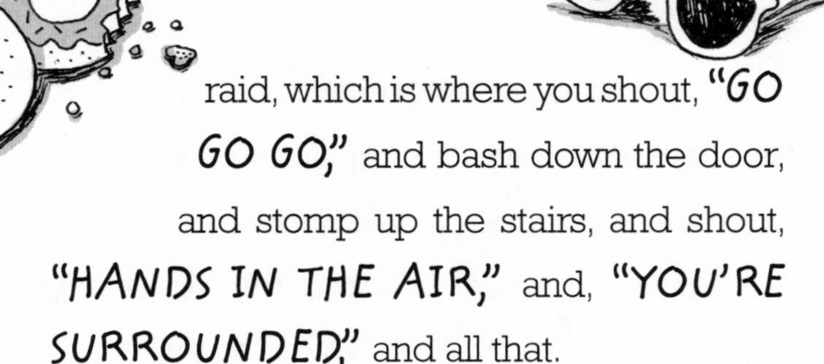

raid, which is where you shout, "GO GO GO," and bash down the door, and stomp up the stairs, and shout, "HANDS IN THE AIR," and, "YOU'RE SURROUNDED," and all that.

And then we made a list of things to take with us.

Anna's And Suzanne's And Tom's
Plan To ~~Steak out~~ Stakeout
The Cat Lady's House

Things We Will Need:

1. Coffee and doughnuts (because that's what Suzanne said the police always have in stakeouts)
2. Binoculars
3. Sunglasses (for a disguise)
4. Watch (so we know how long we've been looking for)
5. Notepad and pen

6. Gardening gloves and Cat Carrier in case we find the New Cat

What We Will Do:

1. Watch the house

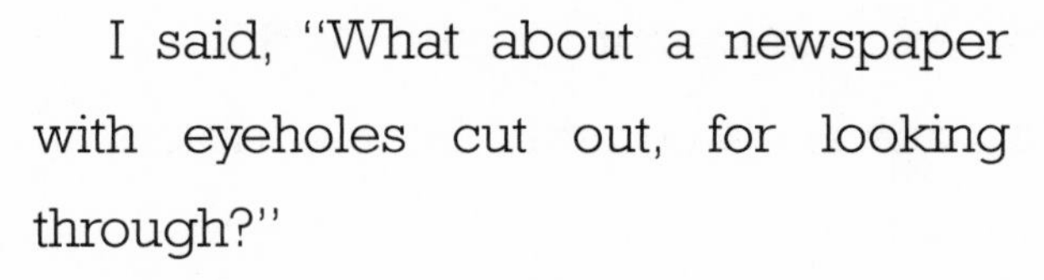

I said, "What about a newspaper with eyeholes cut out, for looking through?"

But Suzanne said, "You don't have those in a *real* stakeout, Anna. That's just in cartoons, actually."

I hate it when Suzanne says "actually," so I said, "Well, some things that happen in cartoons happen in real life as well, actually."

And Suzanne said, "Like what?"

And I couldn't think of anything so I said, "Lots." And then I said, "It's not like you know everything about stakeouts."

And Suzanne said she did, actually.

And I said I didn't think so, because

she didn't even know how to spell it. And that's why she had put an "e" in the middle, which is a piece of meat, like you eat for your dinner.

Suzanne said how you didn't have to be able to spell things to know how to do them. And I said that you did. And Suzanne said, "Then how come I can do a triple side somersault?"

And I said, "You can't. Because I've seen you try and it's just like three wrong-way-round forward rolls."

And Suzanne said it wasn't three wrong-way-round forward rolls, and she wasn't going to do the plan for finding out about the New Cat or anything until I admitted that she could do a triple somersault, and that she knew all about stakeouts. And I didn't say anything. And after ages, I said, "Sorry." But only very quiet, and fast, and with my fingers crossed behind my back.

CHAPTER 14

The Cat Lady's House

Me and Tom and Suzanne stood behind the stone cross in the middle of the marketplace, and peered round, and watched the house through the binoculars.

"Oh, *look*!" Suzanne said. And she passed them to me.

Part of the window had been cleaned, and one of the Missing Pet posters I had dropped, with the picture of the New Cat, had been put in the place where the dirt was wiped away. The sign about the cats not being forced to sit there was still on the window ledge. And the cats were there as well.

And not just three of them, one in each box; this time there were six. And one got up and stretched, and looked out the window, and scratched itself. And then it jumped down behind the curtain, so we couldn't see it anymore. And then another cat came up, from under the curtain, and pushed its way into one of the boxes, and fell asleep.

"How many cats are there?" Tom said.

And Suzanne said, "We'd better keep track." And she got the notepad out and wrote a number for each cat down the side of the page, and wrote what each one looked like beside it, like this:

cat number	looks like
1	ginger, fat
2	black with bits of white
3	Siamese, skinny
4	tortoiseshell, bits out of its ears, one funny eye

We kept count of the cats like that as they came and went from behind the curtain. Tom was the best at spotting them.

And it was me who said if they had any marks that made them stand out, so we would know it again, like, "black paws," or "a piece missing out of its left ear," or "three legs." And Suzanne added them onto the list.

And, after a bit, we took turns eating our sandwiches, and drinking our juice (which we had instead of the doughnuts and the coffee because Mom said she didn't have any doughnuts, only Kit Kats, and she

wouldn't make us a flask of coffee, and she was starting to get suspicious). And I ate Tom's sandwich as well as mine, because he said he didn't want his, because he only wanted the cookies.

And, after ages, it started to rain, and we had to keep wiping our sunglasses, and we still hadn't seen the New Cat, even though we had twenty-three others in the notepad.

And then Suzanne said, "Let's stop the stakeout for today," because it was getting too dark to see the cats, and if she wasn't back for her dinner, she would get in trouble off her Dad. So we started to pack up. And just when we were about to go, something gray shot up into the window, from behind the curtain, and pounced on the tail of the cat with three legs,

which had been hanging down over the window ledge. And the three-legged cat fought back. And then all the cats went mad, and started attacking one another. And you couldn't tell what cat was which; you could just see fur and eyes and teeth and claws.

Tom said, "That was *it*, Anna. That was the *New Cat*."

Tom wanted to go and knock on the door and ask if he could take the New Cat home.

But Suzanne said that wasn't what you did in stakeouts, because then the person being staked would know what was going on, and then Tom would have Blown Our Cover.

Tom said, "Oh." And then, "I think I'll go anyway." Because you can't really stop Tom once he has decided to do something.

And he came out from behind the cross, and ran across the road, and knocked on the door. Just like that. No one answered. So he rang the bell. But no one came.

Suzanne looked through the binoculars. And then Tom walked round the side of the house. And started opening the gate. So me and Suzanne came out from the stakeout spot, and ran after him.

When we got there, Tom was already in the back garden.

"It's a bit messy," he said. Which it was. There was an old mattress, and a sofa, and a frying pan. And lots of things that don't normally go in the garden. And there were more cats as well.

Tom knocked on the back door. We heard a noise, from behind it.

"Someone's coming," Suzanne said.

"Quick," I said. *"Run!"* And I started to go.

But Suzanne and Tom didn't follow, and when I looked back, there was just a big ginger cat, coming out of the cat flap.

Tom said, "I'm about the same size as that cat. Maybe I could get through the cat flap," and he put his head through it. And then he tried to get his shoulders in. But they wouldn't fit. So he took off his coat and tried again. And then he took off his Spider-Man suit with the built-in muscles.

And me and Suzanne got The Hysterics, watching Tom trying to get in, because he looked pretty funny just in his shoes and his underwear.

And then we stopped having The Hysterics because Tom was gone. And we hadn't really thought he could actually get

inside. Because Tom has tried to get in the cat flap at home, lots of times, and he always gets stuck. We looked in through the back windows, but they were too dirty to see through, and there were all sorts of things piled up behind them.

We banged on the back door, and ran round the front, and rang on the bell, and I shouted, "TOM!"

And then Suzanne started saying how it was her dinnertime, again, and how she would get in trouble off her Dad if she was late and all that.

And I said, "We can't leave." Because what if Tom was tied up, or trapped, or dead? And because I was supposed to be looking after him, and we were only supposed to be in the shed.

And then I saw Tom's head coming out through the cat flap. And he wriggled his shoulders through. And he said, "She's too busy looking for something now. And then she has to go shopping. We have to come back for the New Cat another time."

And Suzanne said, "Who?"

And Tom said, "The Cat Lady."

Suzanne looked at her watch. "Let's go," she said.

And there wasn't time for Tom to put his Spider-Man suit on, so he just did the first snap up, on his coat, and he didn't put his arms in, so it looked like a cape. And we ran home. Our fastest.

When me and Tom got in, we could hear Suzanne's Dad through the wall. Shouting about the time, and

Suzanne's dinner, and how it was cold.

Mom wanted to know where me and Tom had been, and why Tom only had his coat on.

"In the shed," I said.

But Mom said she had checked. And then she asked Tom. And Tom said how we had been to the Cat Lady's house, and done a stakeout and Blown Our Cover and all that. And how we had seen the New Cat. And how he got in through the cat flap. And Mom wasn't pleased. Because she said how she had told us already about poking about in other people's property, and we were not to do it. And under no circumstances should we go in through other people's cat flaps.

Tom said, "But what about the New Cat?"

Mom said that after dinner she would go and knock on the door herself, and ask if the lady had the New Cat, and if she did, she would bring it back.

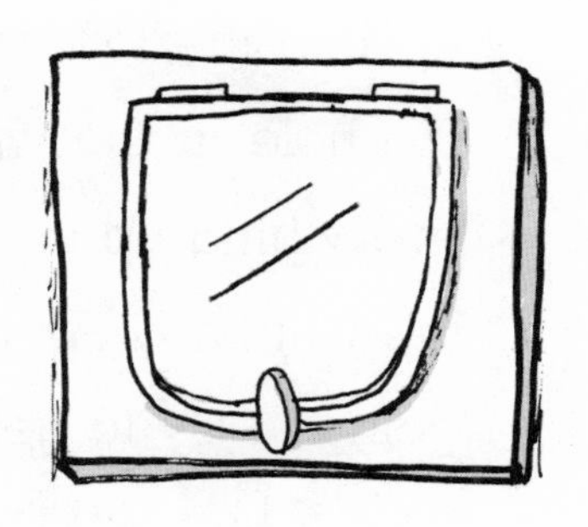

Me and Tom were waiting on the stairs when Mom got back.

"Did you get the New Cat?" Tom said.

"No," said Mom. "Nobody answered." And then she said, "I don't want you going down to that house again. It doesn't look safe." And then she said how we had to come home straight from school every day, and we weren't to go out of the road on our own again unless she said. Mom said she would call at the house again, later in the week, and maybe someone would be home then, and she would ask about the New Cat then.

When everyone was in bed, Suzanne knocked three times on the wall. And I knocked three times back, and we climbed

up into the loft, and across the beams, to the hole in the wall, and we talked about everything up there, like the New Cat and the Cat Lady. And how Mom said she was going to try to get the New Cat back. And how, if she didn't, we could say we were going to Sunday School again next week, and go back ourselves.

CHAPTER 15

The New Cat's New Home

Mom went down to the Cat Lady's house three times, but she never came back with the New Cat.

And the Cat Lady had told Tom we had to come back another time. So when Sunday came round, we told Mom we were going to Sunday School. Which was nearly true because Sunday School was very nearby. And if we got the New Cat back, like Suzanne said, we could go to Sunday School afterward.

We went round the back of the Cat Lady's house, and Tom squeezed in through the cat flap again. And he opened the back door. And me and Suzanne went inside.

It was dark in the Cat Lady's house. And it didn't smell very nice, a bit like the Real Smelling Cesspit, at the Viking Center, where we went on the school trip.

It was even messier inside the house than it was in the garden. There were boxes, and books, and hats, and papers, and picture frames in piles against all the walls. And there was a bald mannequin, and a broken coat stand, and a stuffed deer's head, and some dead flowers in the sink.

Suzanne said, "Is this the kitchen, do you think?"

I said I wasn't sure because it was hard to tell, because if there was an oven, or a dishwasher, or a fridge, they must have been hidden under piles of things. It was like the Brownie jumble sale, before Brown Owl has sorted everything into stalls for clothes, and bric-a-brac, and white elephant, and all that, when all the trash bags have been emptied into the middle of the floor. Only it was more like a hundred Brownie jumble sales. Because some of the piles went right up to the ceiling.

We heard some rustling, and a crashing sound coming from the next-door room.

"That's her," Tom said. And he opened the door, and looked through. "Hello?"

"Send them away, Polly," a voice said. "I'm not inclined to receive this Sunday."

And then there was more rustling and banging and crashing. And a saucepan with no handle came whizzing past, and then a shoe, and then a stuffed owl, which hit Suzanne on the head.

"Ow," Suzanne said.

The Cat Lady came out from a pile of things, backward, and she was coughing from the dust, and she turned round and saw us standing in the door. She looked frightened. "What do you want?"

"Our cat," said Tom.

"How did you get in here? Did Polly let you in?"

"No," said Tom. "I came in through the cat flap."

"Ah, in that case, I apologize. If it's small enough to get in by itself, it's small enough to stay, that's what I say. I had thought you were someone else." And then she whispered, *"Someone official."* And she looked around her in case anyone was listening. "I should have known by your height, I suppose, but they start them so young these days, and they're often undernourished. A policeman knocked lately, and if it wasn't for his hat, I'd have sworn he was the paperboy."

And then the Cat Lady put her hand to her forehead. "I was looking for something, just now, and I can't remember what

it is. . . . Do excuse me a moment. . . ."

And she went into another pile of things, and she rummaged around, and started throwing things out behind her from inside it. And one of them was a pile of our "Missing" posters, about the New Cat.

Suzanne picked up one of the posters and said, "This is the cat we're looking for."

The Cat Lady stopped looking for a moment. "You've lost something, have you? How frustrating. I was looking for something myself just now, only I've quite forgotten what it is."

Suzanne held out the poster. The Cat Lady looked at the picture. "Ah, it's not an affectionate animal, but a marvelous mouser."

The fat ginger cat, which we had seen last time coming out the cat flap, started

rubbing itself against the Cat Lady's legs. "I don't encourage them—the cats—you understand. They just come. But, once they're here, it would be awfully rude not to offer them something. Some of them have traveled."

And then she tipped a big bag of dried cat food onto the floor, and all the cats came round, and started eating it. And the ginger cat ate the most. And he guarded his patch, and if the other cats came near, he went for them. And in about a minute, the food was all gone. And the cats went back to their places.

"They're all in good health, though, as you can see."

They didn't look in good health to *me*. They were the skinniest, scraggiest cats I'd ever seen. Apart from the fat ginger one.

The Cat Lady said, "He's been with me from the beginning. He was a mouser too, in his youth, but now, as you see, he's gone to fat. I've had to enlarge the cat flap. But I'm forgetting myself—do forgive me—it's been so long since we've had company. Will you take some tea?"

Suzanne said, "Yes, please."

The Cat Lady pulled a little bell out of her pocket, and she rang it, and she looked up, like she was waiting for someone to come, and she shook her head and said, "She sleeps so late these days. And who can blame her, of course, a whole life spent in service. Well, if we're to make it ourselves, we shall almost certainly require a kettle. You can never find one when you need one, and when you don't, of course, there's ten all at once. . . ." And she started looking through the piles again.

She didn't find a kettle, but she spotted the saucepan without the handle that had gone whizzing past Suzanne's head, and she said, "Aha. Here we are."

And she went outside and filled it from the outside tap by the back door. And she came back in, and lit a camping stove. And she boiled the water on that. And she said, "If I'd known you were coming, I'd have had Polly bring out the best china." And she rang her little bell again. And she listened. And then she banged with a broom handle on the ceiling, but no one answered.

"Deaf as a post. I should replace her, I suppose, but she's *not quite right,* and who else would take her?"

She rooted around inside her pocket,

and brought out two tea bags, and she dropped them into the saucepan. Then she picked up four empty yogurt pots, and she tipped them upside down, and a few dead flies fell out, and she blew the dust off, and wiped them on her skirt.

"This set is quite serviceable. Came down to me on Mother's side, if I remember rightly." And then she brought two stools over, and two boxes, from a heap behind the front door, and a crate, which she turned upside down for a table. And she poured the tea into the yogurt pots. And we all sat down. And she said, "After you," to Suzanne, and Suzanne said, "After you," to me.

I didn't really want it to be "after me" because the tea didn't look very nice, and there wasn't any milk, and because mine still had half a dead fly in it. But I drank some anyway. Which burned a bit because the tea was very hot, and the yogurt pot was starting to melt.

Tom said, "Have you got any cookies?"

"Cookies, cookies, now where would she keep such a thing?"

She rang the little bell again, and shouted, "Polly," up the stairs. And she started throwing things out behind her, from in the piles again. Until she spotted something on the floor, in the corner, and said, "Aha. The very thing." Which it wasn't really, because it was a beer coaster, but she gave it to Tom, and he bit it, and then he put it down.

And he said, "Can we look for the New Cat now?"

And the Cat Lady said, "Of

course, of course, it is so frustrating when one loses something." And she took three candles out of her pocket, and lit them, and gave us one each to hold. "Mother never held with electricity, and as time passes, I find myself more and more in agreement. It's terribly unforgiving. I shan't come upstairs with you, if you don't mind. I never do, these days. I do hope you find your cat. I was looking for something myself, just now, and I've quite forgotten what it is. . . ." And she went rooting through a pile again.

We started going upstairs.

And the Cat Lady called after us, "Do excuse the papers and so on, which aren't quite organized. My filing system is not what it was, and Polly has grown quite hopeless. Still, no one was ever hurt by a little untidiness."

And it *was* untidy upstairs, too. Even more untidy than downstairs. And more untidy than my and Tom's bedrooms were, the week that Mom went away when Dad was in charge. And more untidy than the shed, and the closet under the stairs. And the pile of Dad's broken things up in the loft.

Because you couldn't see the carpet, except for in little paths, through the piles, and it was so dirty that your feet stuck to it, and you couldn't tell what color it was. And you had to be careful not to knock into anything because, once, when Tom did, a whole pile of things collapsed, and clouds of dust came up, and cats scattered, and boxes, and a long lamp, and a set of brass fire irons, came crashing down, and nearly hit Suzanne on the head. Some of the rooms were so full we couldn't even open the door to look inside.

We searched in all the rooms we could get into, but we didn't see the New Cat. It was quite hard to see *anything* with the candles, and the mess, and all the curtains being closed. After a while we started back downstairs. Suzanne went first. And me and Tom followed, and as we got near the bottom, when Suzanne put her foot forward, to tread onto the last step, something pounced on it, in the dark, with all its claws out, and it dug them right in, and sank its teeth into her ankle.

And Suzanne screamed, "Agh!" and kicked her leg in the air. And the thing flew off, and hit the wall.

"It's the New Cat!" Tom said.

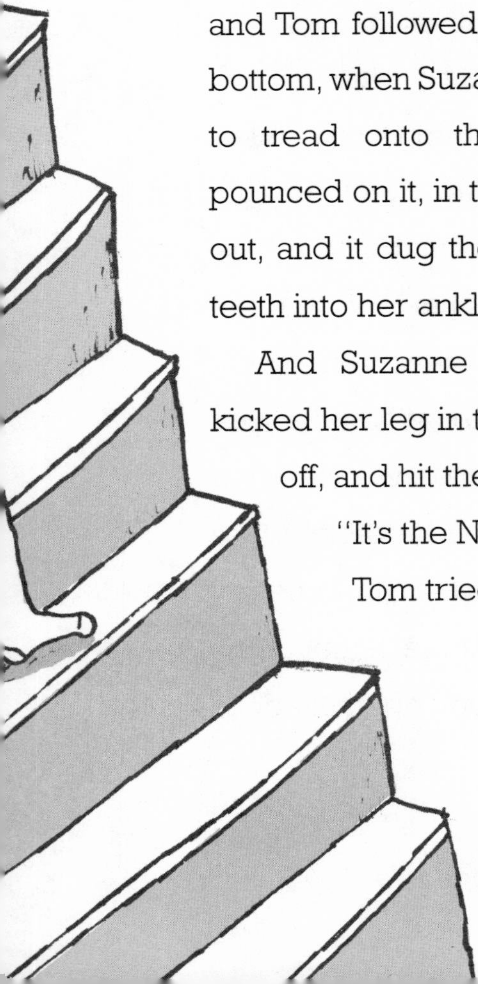

Tom tried to pick the New Cat up, and its ears went flat, and its fur went big, and it scratched, like it always does.

So we went and got the gardening gloves, and the cat carrier. And we got the New Cat into a corner, and we shooed it into the cat carrier. And we took it to show the Cat Lady.

"A cause for celebration," she said. "I suppose champagne would be too much, at this hour, and a Sunday after all. And heaven only knows where Polly might have put it. But will you take some more tea?"

I didn't want any more tea, and nor did Tom and Suzanne. "No thanks," we said.

The Cat Lady looked disappointed. "Have you got any stories instead?" Tom said. "Because we could celebrate with one of those."

"I suppose you know the story of the Cat That Walked By Himself?"

Tom said, "No."

And the Cat Lady said, "Shall we have that one, then?"

And Tom said, "Yes." And we sat down.

And the Cat Lady lit some more candles, and even the cats went quiet, and she said, "HEAR and attend and listen; for this befell and behappened and became and was, O my Best Beloved, when the Tame animals were wild. The Dog was wild, and the Horse was wild, and the Cow was wild, and the Sheep was wild, and the Pig was wild—as wild as wild could be—and they walked in the Wet Wild Woods by their wild lones."

And after a while the Cat Lady stopped, and put her hand up to her forehead, and said, "Oh, I've just remembered, I was looking for something, wasn't I, just now, and I've quite forgotten what it is. . . . Do excuse me. . . ."

And she went into one of the piles, and started looking through it.

And me and Tom and Suzanne went out the back door and went home, with the New Cat, with its ears flat, in the carry case.

CHAPTER 16
Shopping

We opened the front door, and let the New Cat out of the cat carrier, and shooed it inside, and Suzanne took the carry case and the gardening gloves and put them back in the shed.

When Mom saw the New Cat, she said, "Where on earth did you find it?"

"At Church," I said, before Tom said anything. Because even though I told Tom about a million times that he shouldn't say

anything to Mom about being in the Cat Lady's house, and all that, because we're banned, Tom isn't always very good at lying, because sometimes he forgets, and tells the truth by mistake.

The New Cat sat still in the corridor, and looked around. And then it ran into the kitchen, and straight out the cat flap.

"Oh," said Tom.

I said, "Maybe it's gone hunting and it'll be back in a bit."

But it wasn't. And it didn't come back all week.

So when Sunday came around, me and Tom told Mom we were going to Sunday School again, and we called on Suzanne, and we went back to the Cat Lady's house instead.

Tom went in through the cat flap, and let

me and Suzanne in, just like last time, and we told the Cat Lady how the New Cat had gone missing.

And the Cat Lady pointed to the corner where the New Cat was after a mouse.

Suzanne tried to get the New Cat away from the mouse, because it was still a bit alive, and the New Cat went mad, and shot up the curtains, and upset one of the piles, and sent all the cats scattering. And the other cats started attacking one another, and you could just see fur and eyes and teeth and claws. And the mouse got away, through a hole in the floor.

The Cat Lady tipped a bag of cat food into the middle of the floor, and the cats all came round, and started eating. Except the New Cat, which was staring at the hole where the mouse had gone.

Me and Tom and Suzanne closed in on

the New Cat, and got it into the cat carrier, and closed the door. And the New Cat watched the mouse hole through the mesh.

And we sat down on the crates, and Tom asked the Cat Lady to tell us the next bit in the story.

And the Cat Lady lit some candles and told us some more about the Cat That Walked By Himself.

And after that we took the New Cat home again. And this time we pushed it in through the cat flap, like it had come back on its own. And then we went in ourselves and put the lock on. And we put some pieces of ham in the New Cat's dish and the cream off the top

of the milk. And it had a nap, in its basket, with one eye open. And when it woke up, it tried to get out the cat flap, but it couldn't because of the lock, so it just banged its head. And after that it went and waited by the front door, and as soon as someone opened it, which was Mom to let Pam in, the New Cat ran through it.

After that, Suzanne said that she didn't think there was much point in getting the New Cat into the cat carrier every week, and getting all bitten and scratched, and bringing it back. Not if it was only going to run away again. Which was probably true.

And Tom said that, next time, he didn't mind if we just visited the New Cat at the Cat Lady's house, and took the gardening gloves so he could stroke it, and listened to the rest of the Cat Lady's story.

The next Sunday, after Tom had stroked

the New Cat, the Cat Lady asked, "Does anyone fancy a spot of shopping?"

Tom said, "Yes." Because he loves going to the shops, even when it's just the butcher's and the greengrocer's and all that. Because he carries a bag, and sits up on the counter, and dips his wellies in the horse trough on the way past.

I don't like shopping, not like Tom, because normally it's pretty boring, unless it's for sweets. So I said, "What will we be shopping for?"

"We can hardly know until we find it," said the Cat Lady.

Which is different from going shopping with Mom, because she always knows exactly what she's shopping for, because she has it on a list, on the side of the fridge, that says "milk" and "bread" and "braising steak."

But the Cat Lady went past all the food shops, and she went in the charity shop instead. She looked around, and picked things up, and asked the man, "How much is this?" about things. Even though they all had the price on the bottom.

And the man told her, and then the Cat Lady said, "Dear, oh dear, that's daylight robbery." Even about a whole set of cutlery for fifty pence. And then she said, "We shall go elsewhere."

And after that we went into the park, and along by the river, and the Cat Lady said, "Keep your eyes peeled." And she poked in the bins, and then we saw a Dumpster, and the Cat Lady got quite excited. And there were all

sorts of things in there that somebody didn't want, like a broken toilet seat, and a tap with no knobs, and a big rusty hinge.

And me and Suzanne found a few things we thought the Cat Lady would like. Like a can to put her trash in, and some net curtains that looked brand new, and four china cups, which were hardly chipped at all. But the Cat Lady said, "You take them. That's not the kind of thing I need."

And then Tom found a bag of jam-jar lids, all different sizes, and a leg off a chair, and a pair of glasses with the glass missing, which only had one arm. And he showed them to the Cat Lady.

And the Cat Lady said, "Marvelous. Well, what a wonderful eye you have." And she put them straight into her cart. And when the cart was full, she said, "That's enough for today."

And we went back to the house.

Tom and the Cat Lady looked through the things that they had collected. And they found places to put them. And they were both pretty pleased. And the Cat Lady made us some tea, and Suzanne got the china cups out, which we had found. And I gave Tom the cookie I brought from home. And we lit the candles, and sat down. Tom stroked the New Cat with the gardening gloves. And the Cat Lady carried on the story about the Cat That Walked By Himself.

"And the Cat walked by himself, and all places were alike to him. Of course the Man was wild too. He was dreadfully wild. He didn't even begin to be tame till he met the Woman, and she told him that she did not like living in his wild ways. She picked out a nice dry Cave, instead of a heap of wet leaves, to lie down in; and she strewed clean sand on the floor; and she lit a nice fire of wood at the back of the Cave; and she hung a dried wild-horse skin, tail down, across the opening of the Cave; and she said, 'Wipe your feet, dear, when you come in, and now we'll keep house.'"

CHAPTER 17
The Letters

After that we went to the Cat Lady's house every Sunday. And some days we got up early and went before school, too. And sometimes we said that we were staying behind after school for Homework Club, and went then as well.

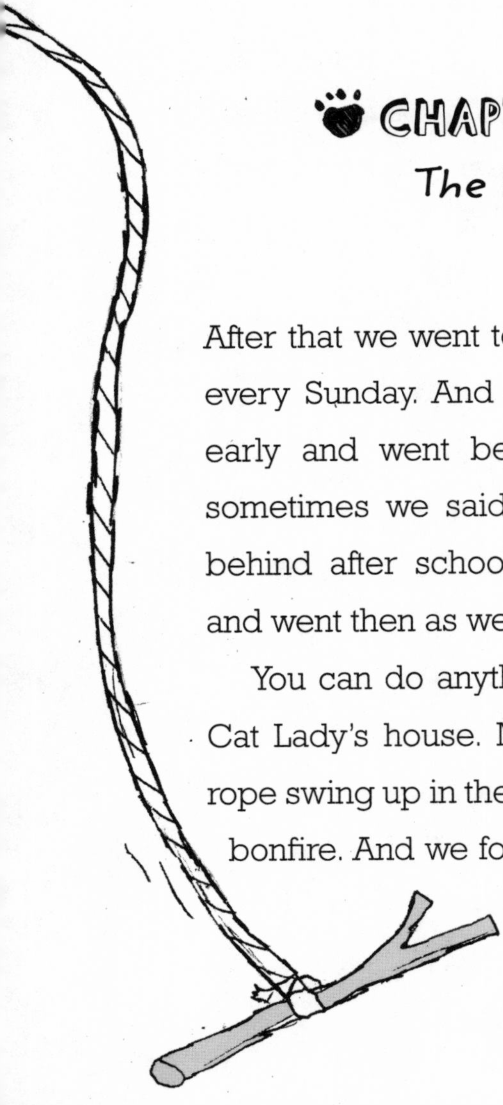

You can do anything you want to at the Cat Lady's house. Me and Suzanne put a rope swing up in the garden. And we built a bonfire. And we found a bag full of tins of sardines and cooked them outside on the camping stove.

Once, when we were there, the doorbell rang. The Cat Lady froze. "Shh," she said, "it's them."

Me and Suzanne got down on our knees, and looked over the window ledge, through the net curtains. There was a man and a woman, in suits. They rang the bell again. And they waited. And then the man put a letter through the letter box. And they went away.

Suzanne went to the door and pulled the letter from the pile of things in front of it and gave it to the Cat Lady.

"I can't imagine where poor Polly will find the time to deal with all this correspondence," the Cat Lady said. "She's not educated, of course, but Mother took care to see she knew her letters, and even in ill health, her handwriting is immaculate."

She put the letter in a bag with

lots of others. And then she said, "Are we shopping?"

And Tom said, "Yes."

But Suzanne said, "I think me and Anna will wait here and help Polly."

And the Cat Lady looked pleased. And me and Suzanne were pleased too, because we didn't really like going down the river-bank, and looking for bits of rubbish, and getting things out of Dumpsters and trash cans, not like Tom. Shopping with the Cat Lady was Tom's favorite thing.

When they had gone, Suzanne went and got the bag full of letters. And she tipped them out, onto the floor, and she counted them all. There were forty-four. And none of them had ever been opened.

Suzanne said, "Let's put them all in order."

So we did, by the dates on the envelopes,

which said when they had been mailed.

And we laid them all out in a long line on the floor. And some of the letters were from three years ago.

"I wonder what they're about?" Suzanne said. And so did I.

"Maybe we should open one."

"Just one," said Suzanne.

So we did. This is what the first letter said:

Dear Mrs. Neville,

We have received numerous complaints relating to the buildup of refuse in the garden to the rear of your property, including several dozen black trash bags, a double mattress, two Chesterfield sofas, and a fridge/freezer. This is a formal request that these items be removed, and the garden cleared to a reasonable standard. Should you require help with the clearance, please contact us at the above number.

Yours sincerely,

Mr. A. Grabham
Senior Environmental Health Officer

And then we opened another one, from the same person, also about the garden, saying it had got worse, and how more people had complained, and asking if the Cat Lady would like someone from the council to come to her house and help her.

And then, after a year, there was one that said:

Dear Mrs. Neville,

An examination of the exterior of your property, and a partial examination of the interior (through the rear windows), has found that its condition threatens both your own health and that of other property occupiers in the immediate vicinity. In particular, we are concerned to find evidence of rats and mice in and around the property (despite the presence of at least twelve cats). We also observed rotting food items and large quantities of animal waste, both inside and outside your property, as well as generally unsanitary and unsafe conditions.

As stated in previous correspondence, failure to keep your property clean, and clear of accumulations of refuse, presents a risk to public health, and, as such, if the current situation does not improve, the council will intervene. Please contact us to arrange for assistance in this matter.

And there were letters giving times and days when people from the council would be coming to talk to the Cat Lady. And others asking to make an appointment. And there were leaflets about "Health and Well-Being in Your Home," and "Caring and Support Services in Your Community," with questionnaires for the Cat Lady to say whether they were "very useful" or "quite useful," or "not very useful," "not at all useful," or whether she was "unsure."

And me and Suzanne filled in the questionnaires, to post back. And we ticked the "unsure" box. And then we were down to the last letter, which was the one that had just arrived. It said:

> Dear Mrs. Neville,
>
> We have attempted to work with you to improve the repair and condition of your property. However, this approach has not resulted in improvements. We therefore see no alternative but to carry out works ourselves. We shall require access to the property over several consecutive days, with as many return visits as deemed necessary, in order to clear it of refuse and restore it to a reasonable standard for habitation. If we do not hear from you with alternative dates, we shall arrive to commence the clearance on Monday, October 24.

And that was in a week.

CHAPTER 18
A Reply

After the Cat Lady and Tom got back from shopping, and showed us their things, and we had all had some tea, and Tom stroked the New Cat with the gardening gloves on, and the Cat Lady had told us the next bit of the Cat That Walked By Himself, me and Tom and Suzanne went home.

And Suzanne took the bag full of letters from the council, because we didn't think the Cat Lady would notice. And, like she said, "Somebody better reply." Because a few of them said **"DELIVERED BY HAND"** in red letters on the front, and they looked pretty important. And because we knew that the Cat Lady wouldn't like it if people from the council came to clear her house out, because she doesn't let anyone in, except for the cats, and me and Tom and Suzanne. And because she hates throwing things away, even more than Dad.

So me and Suzanne started writing back, and we put at the bottom "From Polly," even though we had never met her, and like Suzanne once whispered when the Cat Lady was trying to get Polly's attention by banging on the ceiling with the broom handle, "I don't think Polly actually exists." We wrote back whenever we could, in break and lunchtime at school, and in the back of our notebooks when we were meant to be doing math problems,

and at night when we were supposed to be in bed, through the hole in the wall in the loft. And this is what some of the letters said:

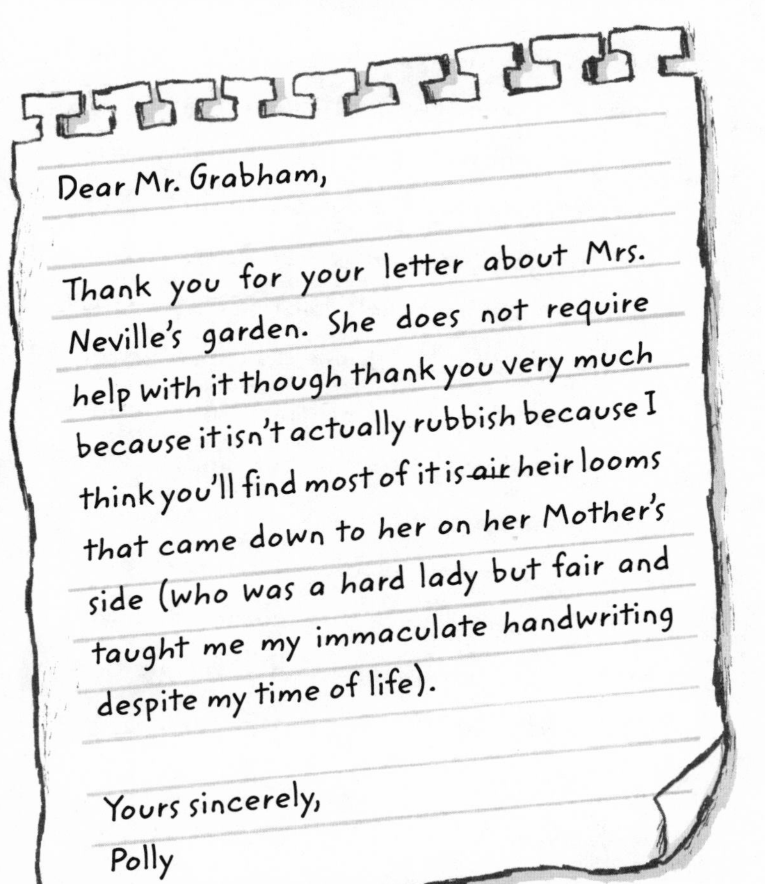
Dear Mr. Grabham,

Thank you for your letter about Mrs. Neville's garden. She does not require help with it though thank you very much because it isn't actually rubbish because I think you'll find most of it is ~~air~~ heir looms that came down to her on her Mother's side (who was a hard lady but fair and taught me my immaculate handwriting despite my time of life).

Yours sincerely,
Polly

Dear Mr. Grabham,

I think it is quite rude to go round looking in people's windows, actually. Especially their rear ones. And that is probably why I keep Mrs. Neville's windows so dirty. Her health is good and so is her cats'. If her neighbors are not well that is not really Mrs. Neville's fault. I hope they get better soon. Have they tried putting their heads over a bowl of boiling water and having some Heinz chicken soup? I have not been quite right myself lately, so I have got a little bit behind with the cleaning. I am better now though and will start picking up the cat poop.

From Polly

Dear Mr. Grabham,

By the time you get this I will have put new curtains up, moved the cat poop, put the dead rats in the trash, and put some flowers that aren't as dead in the window boxes. I hope that this means you do not need to come on October 24. If you do come, Mrs. Neville will be out shopping, and I am sleeping late these days (who can blame me after my life in service?) so I'm afraid you won't be able to get in.

From Polly

And, after that, a new letter came. It said:

Dear Mrs. Neville,

In light of recent correspondence from your employee, Polly, we are arranging for a new inspection of your property. We hope to find the conditions of your property improved significantly. If we do not find these to be sufficient, the clearance of your property will be rescheduled for the following week.

Yours sincerely,

Mr. Grabham

After that, every time Tom and the Cat Lady went out shopping, me and Suzanne did jobs at the Cat Lady's house. We raked the rubbish in the garden and put it into bags, and lit a bonfire, and burned it, and collected all the broken glass. We cleaned the front window, and scrubbed the front step.

It was hard to make things look tidy because there were so many piles of things, and as soon as we put some in the trash or on the bonfire, Tom and the Cat Lady came back with a cart full of new ones.

One time, when Tom and the Cat Lady were out, and I was looking around the house for dead mice and rats, for burying outside, and Suzanne was picking all the cat poop up, and putting them in a trash bag, for burning on the bonfire, the doorbell rang.

Suzanne said, "It might be Mr. Grabham, the council man, come to do the inspection."

We looked out over the

window ledge, through the new net curtain. It wasn't the council man, though. It was Mom.

"*Anna,* I know you're in there."

Me and Suzanne stayed still and didn't say anything. And after a while we heard something out the back, and we went to look out through the cat flap.

Mom was coming up the back garden, past the broken television, and the mattress, and the rolls of chicken wire. And she saw the bonfire, with the rubbish, and the cat poop burning on it, and she saw me and Suzanne looking out through the cat flap.

And she said, "*Home*, now."

I said, "We have to wait for Tom. He's gone shopping."

"Shopping?" Mom said. "Is that what you call it? Tom is home already, Anna."

And she didn't say anything else, all the way home.

Suzanne went into her house. And me and Mom went into ours.

Mom said, "Sit down." And she told me all about how Mrs. Constantine had called round, and how Tom was with her, and how she had found him looking through the trash cans behind the Church with Mrs. Neville.

And how she had asked Mrs. Constantine where I was. And Mrs. Constantine didn't know.

And how Mom asked, "Wasn't she at Sunday School?"

And Mrs. Constantine told her how me and Tom hadn't been to Sunday School for weeks.

And then Mom started shouting, like she never normally does, almost as loud as Suzanne's Dad, and she said, "YOU LIED, ANNA, AND YOU LET TOM GO

OFF WITHOUT YOU, WITH A STRANGER, LOOKING IN TRASH CANS, AND YOU AND SUZANNE HAVE BEEN PICKING UP RATS AND CAT POOP, AND BURNING THEM ON BONFIRES. IT'S A MIRACLE YOU DIDN'T GET TOXOPLASMOSIS, OR WEIL'S DISEASE, OR BURN YOURSELVES ALIVE."

I tried to tell Mom how Tom wasn't with a stranger because he was with the Cat Lady and they had only gone shopping. And me and Suzanne were just trying to tidy up, and how we wouldn't have burned ourselves alive because we know all about fires from Brownies, and Suzanne has got her Fire Safety Badge, and she knows how to escape from a smoke-filled room and everything actually, and Mom said, *"ANNA . . . ,"* like she always does. But louder. *"ENOUGH!"*

And she said that I shouldn't say anything

else. And I should go upstairs. And think about what I'd done.

This is what my dictionary says about toxoplasmosis and Weil's disease:

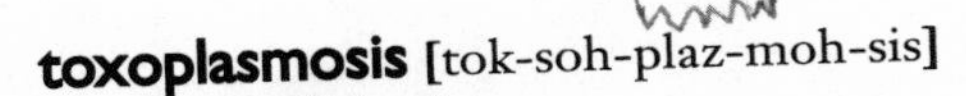

toxoplasmosis [tok-soh-plaz-moh-sis]
✦ *noun (pathology)*
infection with the parasite *Toxoplasma gondii,* transmitted to humans by consumption of insufficiently cooked meat containing the parasite or by contact with contaminated cats or their feces

Weil's [vahylz] ✦ *noun (medical)*
a type of leptospirosis in humans, an infectious disease characterized by fever and jaundice, that damages the liver and kidneys, often caused by bacteria in the urine of rats

CHAPTER 19
The Cat Lady

Me and Suzanne missed going to the Cat Lady's house. But not as much as Tom did, going shopping with the Cat Lady, and stroking the New Cat with the gardening gloves, and hearing about the Cat That Walked By Himself, and all that.

After ages, when Mom stopped being cross, she said if me and Tom wanted, the Cat Lady could come to our house. And she would call round and invite her.

"The Cat Lady won't answer the door," I said.

"I'll pop a note through," said Mom.

"The Cat Lady doesn't open her post," I said, "because she thinks someone called Polly does it, who probably doesn't exist."

But Mom went anyway, and she knocked on the door. And when no one answered, she put a note through, with our address on it, and all that, asking the Cat Lady to come. And she said, "I'm sure she will if she wants to."

But the Cat Lady never came.

After a while, me and Suzanne went back to doing things in the shed, and collecting worms, and making wasp traps, and all that. And Tom went up and down the road collecting gravel, and walking in a straight line with his eyes closed, and picking up litter with Mr. Tucker.

And we didn't do much else because we weren't allowed past the bottom of the road by ourselves. Because Mom said we couldn't be trusted anymore.

Then, one day, which was Tuesday because Suzanne was there, when we were all having our dinner, the cat flap flipped open, and the New Cat came in.

The New Cat looked wilder than ever. And its fur was even more matted, and one of its ears had a bit missing, and it was so skinny you could see the bones in its back.

Mom went and got some cat food and put it in the New Cat's dish, and the New Cat ate it all, really fast, and it kept looking behind it, like one of us might take its food.

And after that it sat on the rug by the radiator. And Tom went and got the gardening gloves, and stroked it. And the

New Cat didn't scratch, or try to get away. It just stayed still, and closed its eyes, and fell asleep.

Tom said, "The New Cat has probably come to see me, because I haven't been to visit, and soon it will go back."

But the New Cat stayed all night. And in the morning, it was still there.

On the way to school, we told Joe-down-the-street all about the New Cat and what had happened, and how it had come back. And Joe said that his babysitter Brian's cat had come back as well.

And at playtime Suzanne asked Emma Hendry if she had found her cat. And she said, "It came back yesterday. All on its own."

When we got home, me and Tom and Suzanne told Mom about how Emma's and Brian's cats had come back.

And Mom said, "How strange, I wonder why."

"We could go down to the Cat Lady's house and see," I said.

And Tom said, "If she doesn't answer the door, I can go in through the cat flap."

And Mom started going on about how you shouldn't go poking round other people's houses, and going in through their cat flaps, and how the Cat Lady's house isn't safe, and all that.

And she said, "I'll go and see if she's all right myself."

When Mom came back, she said, "Nobody's home. There aren't any lights on. Maybe she's visiting relatives. I'll try again tomorrow."

But the Cat Lady never has lights on. Because she doesn't like electricity. And, like Suzanne said, "I don't think she's got any relatives." And Mom going again tomorrow wouldn't make any difference because, like we already told her, the Cat Lady won't answer the door. Me and Tom and Suzanne went out to the shed and started trying to think of reasons why the cats had come back.

Tom said, "I think the New Cat came back to see me."

"I think it came back because it was hungry," Suzanne said. Which was probably true. Because it was thin, and it had only been back for a night, and it had eaten four tins of cat food, three slices of ham, and two of Tom's cookies, which it doesn't normally like.

Suzanne said, "The Cat Lady must have stopped feeding the cats."

"Why would she do that?" I asked.

"What if she ran out of cat food?" Tom said.

And Suzanne said, "What if she just forgot?"

And I said, "What if she's not very well?"

And Suzanne said, "What if she's dead?"

Tom started chewing his sleeve.

"We need to go down and find out," Suzanne said. But, like I told Suzanne, we couldn't do that because of being banned. And because of not being allowed past the bottom of the road on our own. And because ever since everything happened with the Cat Lady, Mom was always coming out and checking where we were, and what we were up to.

"There's no way we can go without Mom noticing," I said.

But Suzanne said, "There might be *one* way." And she reached behind the stepladders, under the shelf with the wasp trap, and the worm box, and she pulled out the plan for going through all the lofts, which we did ages ago, before we started trying to find the New Cat.

The plan wasn't finished, because we had only written the title, which was "Anna's And Suzanne's Plan To Find Out If There Are Holes In All The Walls In All The Lofts In All The Houses In The Road And, If There Are, Whether We Can Climb Through Them And Come Out In The House At The Bottom, Which is Joe-Down-the-Street's." But Suzanne said we should try it anyway. Because she said we could just go up into my bedroom, and Mom wouldn't check on us if we were playing up there. And we could get up inside the loft, and go through all the holes, and come out at the bottom of the road, in Joe's. And then we could run down to the village and check on the Cat Lady, and go back the same way, without Mom knowing we had even left my bedroom.

"It's easy," said Suzanne.

It didn't sound that easy, I didn't think, because for one thing we didn't even know if the lofts *did* all have holes in them, or if they were all joined together. And for another thing when we got to the bottom, the hatch in Joe's house might be closed, and how would we get out?

Suzanne got a flashlight down from the shelf in the shed, and she turned it on, and she said, "Who wants to come?"

And Tom said, "Me." And he put on his Bob the Builder hard hat with the light on the front.

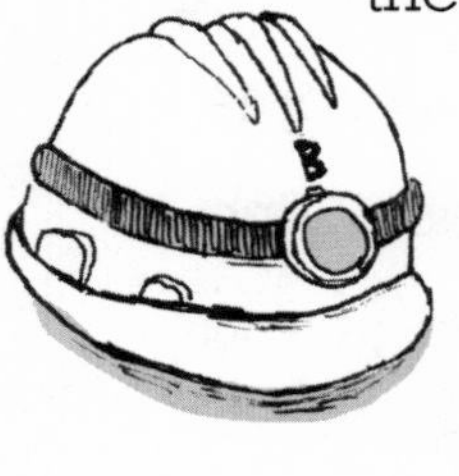

And we went up into my bedroom. And we got up on the chest of drawers, and opened the hatch, and pulled ourselves up into the loft. And we got up onto the beam and balanced on it, and I told Tom how we had to step from one beam to the next. Which was a bit hard. Because Tom's legs are only little. And when we went across, he nearly missed the beam, and slipped, and he grabbed on to Dad's pile of "useful" things, from the closet under the stairs, to stop himself from falling off.

Dad's pile of things wobbled, and the toaster fell off the top, and hit Suzanne on the head.

"Ow," Suzanne said.

And then the whole pile collapsed. And all of Dad's things came down: the bag of worn-out footballs, and the broken tennis rackets, and the pile of newspapers he hasn't got round to reading yet. And the alarm clock that doesn't go off, and the kettle that me and Tom blew up by mistake. And the stool with

one leg,
and a bucket
with a hole in the
bottom, and half
a broom handle
without a head. And
the boxes. And the
bag of clothes
from the olden
days. And it
went right
through the
ceiling.

"Oh,"
Suzanne said.

Me and
Tom and
Suzanne got down on

our hands and knees. And we looked through the hole in the ceiling, down to my bedroom underneath, where all Dad's things were on the floor.

And then Mom came running in, and she looked down at the pile of things on the floor, and she looked up at me and Tom and Suzanne through the hole, and she said, "Are you three all right?"

And I said, "Yes."

And she said *"Anna . . . ,"* like she always does, only a bit angrier, "*come down.*"

And we did. And Mom said how me and Tom and Suzanne had "NO BUSINESS BEING IN THE LOFT." And we were "NEVER TO GO UP THERE AGAIN." And she said, *"DO YOU HEAR ME?!"* And we did. Because she said it quite loud.

And Mom looked at the pile of things

on the floor, and back up at the hole in the ceiling, and she said, *"PETE . . ."*

And Dad came in. And he saw the hole, and all his things, and how they had come through the ceiling. And he said, "Ah, well, the thing *is*, you *see* . . ."

And Mom told me and Tom and Suzanne to go and play outside. So we did. And we could hear Mom talking to Dad from in the front garden. All about his "rubbish," and how she had been asking him to get rid of it for "*ten years,*" and how he was "supposed to have taken it to *the dump,*" and how "SOMEONE COULD HAVE BEEN *KILLED.*" And how now she would have to have a *"WHOLE NEW CEILING!"*

Mr. Tucker was in the road, picking up litter. "Hallo, Bods," he said, "sounds like the Blitz in there."

We told him about how all Dad's things

had fallen through the ceiling. And how Mom was cross. And what had happened with the Cat Lady, and the New Cat, and how it had come back. And how we wanted to go to her house, to check if the Cat Lady was all right, in case she was sick, or dead, or she had run out of cat food or something like that. But we weren't allowed to go past the end of the road on our own.

"Not without a grown-up," Tom said.

Mr. Tucker said, "A grown-up, is it, Basher? And, say you found one? What's the plan on landing, Popsie?"

I said there wasn't really a plan.

"Mmmmm," said Mr. Tucker. "Take a dim view of that, very dim."

"There *is*," said Suzanne, "but we haven't *written* it yet."

"We just want to look," Tom said.

"Quick shufti, is it? Recon, you say? Well,

look here, bit hush-hush, keep it under your hats, but technically speaking, I'm a grown-up myself." Which was true. And Mr. Tucker said he would come with us.

On the way we told him all about the council, and the letters, and how the Cat Lady doesn't answer the door, and how Tom goes in through the cat flap.

And Mr. Tucker said, "Cat flap? Not sure I like the sound of that."

But me and Suzanne told Mr. Tucker how Tom had done it millions of times. And how as soon as he gets in, he opens the back door, and lets us in as well.

And Mr. Tucker said, "All right, aircrew, belt up: briefing. Basher, you're skipper; Old Lag's second Dicky. Popsie and Blondie, Arse-End Charlies." He looked at his watch. "T.O.T. eighteen hundred hours. So, when I give the green, Skipper's off, in through the cat flap, back door open, bang on target, no silly beggars. Any offensive fire, straight out, Old Chap. All clear?"

And me and Tom and Suzanne said it was.

And Mr. Tucker gave us the salute. And we gave him the salute back.

Suzanne opened the gate into the Cat Lady's back garden.

"Good God. Looks like it's been hit for a six. Right-o, Old Chum, got your clobber?"

Tom took his coat off, and switched on the light on his Bob the Builder hard hat.

"Chocks away."

Tom squeezed in through the cat flap.

Me and Suzanne and Mr. Tucker waited.

After a while, Mr. Tucker pushed open the cat flap. "All right in there, Basher?"

"I can't open the door," Tom said. "There's things in the way."

And there were, because Mr. Tucker shone his flashlight in.

There was more stuff than ever. And most of the piles had collapsed. And there wasn't enough room for Tom to turn round.

Mr. Tucker said, "Reverse gear, Basher. Backward. Easy does it."

But Tom didn't come back. He wriggled a bit farther forward.

And Mr. Tucker said, "That's far enough, Old Chum. Come back."

And then we heard a crash.

And Mr. Tucker said, "Basher? Can you hear me, Old Chap?"

But Tom didn't answer.

And Mr. Tucker shook the door handle, and then he leaned against the door, and pushed his shoulder against it. Then he walked down the garden. And when he got to the bottom, he shouted, "Clear the runway. . . ." And he ran at the door, and went straight into it with his shoulder. And the door burst open.

Tom was stuck under some boxes.

Mr. Tucker pulled them off him.

"Look," Tom said. And he pointed to the big ginger cat, which was sitting at the edge of a heap of boxes and papers and things that had collapsed.

Mr. Tucker shone his flashlight over. And he said, "Good God." Because next to the cat, sticking out from under one of the piles of things that had collapsed, was a pair of feet, like happens when the house falls in the *Wizard of Oz*, only without the ruby slippers.

Mr. Tucker picked Tom up, and the big ginger cat. And he carried them both out, and then he took us all to the phone box, and he dialed 999. And said, "Ambulance."

CHAPTER 20
The Hospital

The next day, at school, everyone was talking about the Cat Lady. And how the ambulance had come. And how they had had to smash the front window to get inside. And move mountains of things before they could find her. And how they brought her out on a stretcher, with an oxygen mask on. And put her in the ambulance, with the lights on and the siren. And how it was Tom who had found her. And how Mr. Tucker broke his arm, going in to get Tom. Which was all true. And that's why, after Mr. Tucker took us home, Dad took him to the hospital.

After school, Mom took me and Tom and Suzanne to visit Mr. Tucker. Mr. Tucker was sitting up in bed, with his arm in a sling. And Mom said, "Thank you," again to Mr. Tucker, for saving Tom.

And Mr. Tucker said how it was Tom who was the hero, and how he "ought to get a medal" and all that.

And Mom patted Tom on the head. And gave Mr. Tucker some grapes and said, "I'll be back for you all in an hour."

Mr. Tucker said, "Right Wing: Debriefing."

And we told him all about how the police put cones outside the Cat Lady's house, and tape that said "Keep Out." And how there

were three Dumpsters, and a fire engine, and two vans that said, "Environmental Health," and people in white space suits bringing things out of the Cat Lady's house, in bags that said "Toxic."

And Tom said, "Do you think that the Cat Lady is all right?"

And Mr. Tucker said, "Ask her yourself, Basher." And he pointed to the bed opposite. "Not sure I hold with it. All this mixed ward business." And he gave me the grapes and said, "Take her these. There's only so many a man can eat."

Both the Cat Lady's legs were in plaster, and they were up in the air. And she had lots of bruises from where all the things in the piles had fallen on top of her. And the nurse

told us we should be quiet because the Cat Lady wasn't well, and she was a bit confused, and how they thought she had been trapped on the floor for three days.

The Cat Lady didn't recognize me and Suzanne. But she smiled at Tom. And she patted the bed, beside her, and Tom sat on it. And she stroked him on the head. And Tom gave her the grapes, and asked her to tell us the rest of the story, about the Cat That Walked By Himself, because we never got to the end.

And the Cat Lady said, "Then the Man threw his two boots and his little stone ax at the Cat, and the Cat ran out of the Cave, and the Dog chased him up a tree; and from that day to this, Best Beloved, three proper Men out of five will always throw things at a Cat whenever they meet him, and all proper Dogs will chase him up a tree. But the Cat keeps his side of the bargain too. He will kill mice and he will be kind to Babies when he is in the house, just as long as they do not pull his tail too hard. But when he has done that, and between times, and when the moon gets up and night comes, he is the Cat that walks by himself, and all places are alike to him. Then he goes out to the Wet Wild Woods or up the Wet Wild Trees or on the Wet Wild Roofs, waving his wild tail and walking by his wild lone."

And Mr. Tucker started snoring in the bed opposite.

And then the Cat Lady fell asleep as well.

And me and Suzanne ate the rest of the grapes, and Tom ate Mr. Tucker's cookies, until Mom came to collect us.

CHAPTER 21
Cleaning the Cat Lady's House

That's pretty much everything that happened with Tom, and the Cat Lady, and the Great Cat Conspiracy.

All week people went in and out of her house while the Cat Lady was in the hospital. And they cleared everything out, even the carpets, and the wallpaper, and after they cleaned it, and made it so you could tell what each room was, people came in to paint the walls, inside the house and out, and the window frames, and the front step, and the door. And they put new glass in the windows, and new tiles on the roof. And made the chimney so it didn't look like it was going to fall off. And people said it took twenty-six Dumpsters to take all the things away and make the Cat Lady's house tidy.

On the day the Cat Lady came back from the hospital, Mom came with me and Tom and Suzanne to take her some flowers, and Mr. Tucker came too, with his arm in a sling, and he brought the ginger cat, which Mrs. Tucker had been looking after.

A nurse opened the door.

The Cat Lady was sitting in her front room, and she was looking at the wall. The nurse went into the kitchen to put the flowers in a vase.

And me and Tom and Suzanne and Mom and Mr. Tucker all sat down. On chairs. Because all the boxes and crates had gone.

The Cat Lady looked a bit scared. She was holding her hands tight under her chin. She looked around the room. And she saw her little bell, on the mantelpiece, and she rang it. And she looked up at the ceiling. And, very quietly, she said, "She's deaf as a post. One ought to replace her, but who else would take her, at her time of life?"

And then the nurse came in, and she said, "Can I help?"

The Cat Lady looked scared. "How did you get in here? Did Polly let you in?"

Mr. Tucker said to the nurse, "Prob'ly do with a brew up, I think."

And the nurse nodded her head and went to make some tea.

The Cat Lady looked worried. She put her hand on her forehead. "I was looking for something, just now," she said, "and I can't remember what it is."

She started looking around the room, and wringing her hands.

Tom opened the catch on the cat carrier. The ginger cat walked out, and it went over to the Cat Lady, and rubbed itself against the Cat Lady's legs, in the plaster casts. The Cat Lady picked the cat up, and closed her eyes, and held it tight.

Mom let me and Tom visit the Cat Lady after that. And for six weeks someone brought her meals on wheels and did all her cleaning, and looked after her while her legs were in plaster.

And then, when the Cat Lady got her casts off, the nurses and the helpers stopped coming. And the Cat Lady was pleased because she said, "Polly does everything I need in the house. And I'm quite capable of doing my own shopping."

And sometimes when we went, Mr. Tucker came with us, which the Cat Lady didn't like much, because she said, "How did you get in? Did Polly let you in?"

And Mr. Tucker said, "Spot on, Squadron Leader. Sit tight, shan't stop, quick shufti." And he picked up some rubbish from the corner and put it in his black trash bag.

And the Cat Lady said, "She had no business inviting any old Tom, Dick, or Harry in off the street," and she whispered to her cat, "The man is *quite mad*."

Mr. Tucker said, "That's it, tiggerty-boo, I shall get weaving. Chocks away." And he gave the Cat Lady a salute. And the Cat Lady looked at the wall. And Mr. Tucker went home.

Mr. Tucker came quite often, and picked up the litter in the Cat Lady's garden, and tried to keep things tidy in the house. And

so did me and Suzanne. Because after the nurses and the helpers stopped coming, the Cat Lady started making a little pile of things at the bottom of the stairs, and leaving things in the sink, and once when we went, we couldn't see the kitchen table, and the time after that she had tipped cat food on the floor. And then, one day, we saw, behind the curtain, on the window ledge, there were three fruit boxes, with blankets in, and there was a sign next to them that said, "These cats are not forced to sit here. They do so of their own free will." And, slowly, after that, the cats started coming again.

The End

Have you read the first two investigations?

Available in all good bookshops.